"You've got this survivor thing down to a science, don't you?" he said.

Her heart pounded under his direct, unreadable expression. Why was he doing this to her? He had to know how woefully unprepared she was for a man like him. She parted her lips, not sure if it was to breathe or speak but found it didn't matter, since she could do neither.

"I know all about surviving," he continued. "But we gotta make a decision, and I'm not sure I'm thinking clearly enough to make the right one."

"About what?"

"About whether we're going to remember all the reasons we became survivors in the first place." He leaned closer, tilting his head as if he meant to kiss her. "Or say to hell with it all and finish what we began a few minutes ago."

WHAT ARE *LOVESWEPT* ROMANCES?

They are stories of true romance and touching emotion. We believe those two very important ingredients are constants in our highly sensual and very believable stories in the LOVE-SWEPT line. Our goal is to give you, the reader, stories of consistently high quality that may sometimes make you laugh, sometimes make you cry, but are always fresh and creative and contain many delightful surprises within their pages.

Most romance fans read an enormous number of books. Those they truly love, they keep. Others may be traded with friends and soon forgotten. We hope that each LOVESWEPT romance will be a treasure—a "keeper." We will always try to publish

LOVE STORIES YOU'LL NEVER FORGET
BY AUTHORS YOU'LL ALWAYS REMEMBER

The Editors

WILD
RAIN

DONNA
KAUFFMAN

BANTAM BOOKS
NEW YORK · TORONTO · LONDON · SYDNEY · AUCKLAND

This book is dedicated to my two smallest heroes, my young sons, Mitchell and Spencer. Thank you for being so understanding when Mommy goes off to play with her imaginary friends.

WILD RAIN

A Bantam Book / March 1995

If you would be interested in receiving protective vinyl covers for your Loveswept books, please write to this address for information:

Loveswept
Bantam Books
P.O. Box 985
Hicksville, NY 11802

ISBN 0-553-44469-7

Published simultaneously in the United States and Canada

PRINTED IN THE UNITED STATES OF AMERICA

OPM   0 9 8 7 6 5 4 3 2 1

ONE

The wind screamed in his ears as a burning pain sliced across his thigh. But then, alligators weren't known for their light touch.

"Bloody son of a bitch!"

The moment he'd caught sight of the dark shape hurtling at him in his peripheral vision, Reese Braedon had leapt instinctively into a diving roll. The fierce wind slowed him just enough for the alligator to snag his jeans . . . and his flesh. He came swiftly to his feet, ignoring the heat shooting up his thigh, not taking even a second to examine the extent of his wound. Eyes trained on his attacker, he dropped into a crouch and raised the handgun he'd palmed from his ankle strap while rolling. Needing both hands to steady the weapon in the high wind, his aim nonetheless remained dead center. Right down the throat of the alligator. A very big, very agitated, hissing alligator.

It looked about nine feet long, but Reese was having a hard time getting past its mouth. It was wide open and lined with rows of vicious-looking teeth.

"What's your problem, old bugger?" he asked under his breath. He moved a slow step back. The alligator remained where it was. He took another small step. No movement. But that open mouth and the speed with which the reptile had overtaken him earlier made him more than a little wary.

"Just a simple job," he muttered. "Grab the tart and get her off the island." He took another step. "No one told me she kept an overgrown suitcase with fangs as a watchdog."

When he was a good twenty feet away, he carefully began to straighten. His aim did not waver. "There's a good battler," he cajoled, knowing the alligator couldn't possibly hear him, though he'd let the damn thing eat him alive before admitting the soothing tone was for his own benefit.

When he'd driven over the rickety bridge from Sanibel Island to Caracoles Key, his only concern had been whether Jillian Bonner was going to fall down in gratitude and thank him for saving her from certain death, or whether he was going to have to cart her bodily off the tiny spit of land as her mother seemed to believe would probably be the case.

He didn't much care how he carried out his job. Either way he'd get paid and Mrs. Ravensworth would sleep easy knowing her only child hadn't been swept into the Gulf of Mexico by Hurricane Ivan.

Predictions were flying fast and furious, but no one seemed to question that the storm touted as Ivan the Terrible would live up to its advance billing.

No one except Jillian Bonner. And her damn pet.

The alligator changed things. Now Reese was mad. And when he lost his temper, someone always paid.

He straightened a bit further. "You don't want me, you old codger," he called out, keeping his tone even and grinding his teeth together in what he hoped passed for a smile. "Even the meanest crocs in Australia didn't eat me when they had the chance."

He straightened his legs an inch and took another step back. The alligator maintained its aggressive stance.

Suddenly, out of nowhere, a heavy weight blindsided him, driving into the side of his knees. He hit the ground hard on his chest, but quickly regained his senses. His first thought was that another gator had nailed him from behind, but those were definitely human hands gripping his thighs. A quick glance over his right shoulder showed that the alligator had backed away, as if unsure what to make of this new intruder.

Dismissing that threat for the one literally on his back, Reese expertly flipped up and over, pinning his assailant to the ground between his thighs and leveling his gun on him in one swift move.

Only his attacker wasn't a him.

"What the bloody hell do you think you're doing?" Even though his captive was less than a foot away, he yelled his question at the top of his lungs. Partly to be heard over the howling wind, and partly in complete frustration.

He'd been taken down by a woman! And judging from the fact that he'd barely had to spread his legs to straddle her, not much of one either. He assessed what he could see of her with a swift glance. Short dark hair, smallish dirt-smeared features, bony shoulders, no boobs. Hell, she was more boy than woman.

She grimaced, then surprised him by tugging her hands out from where he'd pinned them to her sides with his knees. She immediately grabbed his thighs and began shoving. He didn't budge.

It belatedly occurred to him that being considerably bigger than she was, he was crushing her. He still didn't move, but his temper curbed. Slightly.

Until her frantic grasping caught him directly on his fresh wound. The hot slash of pain shot up his leg and went straight to his brain. He tossed the gun to the ground, grabbed her hands and pinned them above her head, bringing his own face within an inch of hers. He gave her his fiercest scowl.

"Jillian Bonner?"

She stopped her ineffective attempts at escape and blinked up at him. He was distracted for a split second by her eyes. If asked, he couldn't have said why. They were a nondescript gray. The moment passed as she treated him to a scowl of her own. It was a damn good one too.

For a sheila.

"Yes, I am. Now could you get off me?"

The mouse that roared, Reese thought, fighting the sudden odd urge to smile.

"Please?" The request came through gritted teeth.

Reese continued to stare down at her. Stubborn and tenacious were two of her more obvious traits. Yet it was something else that held his complete attention. There, in the depths of her eyes, was a trace of something . . . Not entirely hard and cold, nor soft and vulnerable. Just the enduring essence of battles fought. Some won. Too many lost. It wasn't blatant or world-weary. But it was there. He knew so, because it was the same thing he saw when he made the mistake of staring too deeply into a mirror.

Like his, hers were the eyes of a survivor.

Maybe they weren't so nondescript after all.

Enough, he decided abruptly. He changed his grip so he could hold her slender wrists in one hand, using the other to scoop up his gun. Tucking it in the waistband of his jeans, Reese lifted his body off her and stood, pulling her to her feet as he went. He paused to run a quick visual check for the alligator, the descending gloom of the storm making it difficult.

"Did you hurt Cleo?" she yelled over the wind. He jerked his gaze around to her. "What?"

"My alligator. Is she hurt?"

"Who the hell—? *Your* alligator?"

She didn't wait around for him to ask questions. In the next instant, with a hard yank, Jillian sprang free and took off racing across the yard.

"The damn thing almost had my leg for lunch and you're worried about how *it's* doing?" he roared after her. His words were swallowed by the wind. She didn't slow a step in her dash to the rear area of the compound.

Swearing under his breath, he took off after her, ignoring the daggers in his thigh as he closed the distance between them. She slowed as she neared a pond. Across the small expanse of water, Reese could make out the hulking shape of the alligator as it hovered near a huge pile of what looked to be earth, leaves, and twigs.

Reese stopped about two feet away. And palmed his gun.

"Jillian!"

She spun around, her expression changing from concern to anger when she spied him. Or rather when she spied his gun.

"Put that thing away! You'll scare her."

"I'll—What? Scare *her*?" Reese knew he was sputtering. He never sputtered. "She's a nine-foot alligator with a bad attitude," he yelled back. "This barely makes things even. No way."

"Did you hurt her?" she demanded again.

"No!" His patience unraveled to its last thread. He could barely believe what he was hearing. She hadn't once asked if he'd been hurt. Not that he intended to tell her. It was obvious she cared more for the damn mutant reptile than she did about a human being. Namely him.

"Let's get the hell out of here before she comes back."

"You sure you didn't shoot her?" She turned her back to him without waiting for his reply. Using her hands to keep her bangs from whipping into her eyes, she squinted as she looked across the pond.

"We haven't got time to waste," Reese shouted.

"Don't let me stop you."

The last thread snapped, and Reese closed the short space between them and grabbed her arm. "Let's go." Without another word, he turned and started toward the house, not bothering to alter his long-legged gait, which, even wounded, kept her trotting beside him to keep up.

Now that he was no longer under attack—from woman or beast—he turned his thoughts back to his original plan. Getting Jillian Bonner off this island and to safety before the hurricane hit. He didn't spare a thought as to whether she'd go along with that plan. He'd promised Regina Ravensworth he'd get her daughter away from danger. And he kept his promises. All he had to do was get a few of her things packed and they were out of there.

He'd gone about five yards when she abruptly

dug in her heels and yanked hard at the hand gripping her wrists. He stumbled, sending a fresh rush of pain up his leg, but didn't let his hold on her wrists slacken enough for her to break free. Biting back several oaths, he spun around to face her but she cut him off before he'd uttered his first word.

"Excuse me," she yelled, "but just who in the hell do you think you are?"

"The only idiot stupid enough to risk his life to save your scrawny butt," he yelled back, wondering just how he'd lost control of this supposedly simple operation.

"Well, nobody asked you to! Let me go!"

Any other time he'd have admired her grit. Now it merely frustrated the daylights out of him. Didn't she know that one hundred and fifty miles per hour of rage and fury were about to come down on her?

"When we're in the house," he shouted back, and turned toward the front door.

She dug in her heels again, making him drag her awkwardly for several feet. "You're not going into my house. This is private property!" When he didn't slow down, she tugged again and yelled even louder. "I'm not going anywhere with you. I demand that you leave immediately!"

That snapped it. He whirled on her so fast, she smacked against his chest. He bent low and shoved his face right into hers so there would be no doubt she would hear what he was about to say.

"I intend to. Just as soon as you grab whatever

you plan on saving." She opened her mouth to speak, but he talked right over her. "Don't push me or I'll throw you over my shoulder and the hell with your precious mementos."

"Aren't you taking this evacuation thing a bit far?" Her glare proved she wasn't the least bit intimidated by his threat. "I told the guys who came by yesterday that I wasn't leaving. Last time I checked, it was my choice."

"Yeah, well, you hadn't checked with me. Now let's move." Reese didn't wait for a response. He swung around and pulled her—dragged her really —toward the porch. It wasn't until he'd gone halfway up the steps of the Victorian-style home that he realized the front door had been shut off with galvanized steel sheets. As he backtracked to the gravel pathway, he noticed the same measures had been taken with the upper-story windows.

Well, at least she'd had enough sense to take some decent precautions. Not that it was going to help. Hurricane Ivan was likely to turn her house into a pile of kindling—with or without steel window covers. He headed around the side of the house, figuring she must have come out that way.

"I really must insist," she tried again.

Reese ignored her as he spied the small screened-in sun porch. He went straight through, not stopping until they were standing in her kitchen. He turned to face her. With the door shut, the howling wind was substantially muted, and the sudden lack of noise made his ears ring. He ignored that too. He'd blanked out far worse in his life.

Still holding her wrists, he said, "You have five minutes. Important papers, family stuff, some clothes. I'll turn off your utilities. Where is the fuse box?"

She stood there, gaping at him.

He fought the urge to shake her. From her mother's description, he'd expected some mousy professor type. He realized he hadn't believed Mrs. Ravensworth, a high society matron with the sort of timeless beauty that had men decades younger drooling.

But Jillian was all that her mother described and worse. The only unexpected element being her fierce reaction to him. Quiet, very reserved, a loner, were the adjectives Regina had used. She'd also said her daughter could be very stubborn about certain things. Namely, her home and the animals in her care.

After all the yelling and glaring, he wasn't certain he agreed with the first part, but he'd been given ample proof of the latter.

Not that it made any difference. Her mother had been right about the most important thing. Her size. Negligible. And last he checked he was still a steady one ninety-five.

No contest.

"I'm not—"

"Four minutes, thirty seconds."

"Leaving," she finished stubbornly. She pulled

her wrists free and massaged them, glowering at him with those plain gray eyes.

He felt a strange twinge, like he should apologize or something. He ignored it. It wasn't his fault she was making it difficult on herself.

He looked down at her. She was a good six or seven inches shorter than he, hardly filling out the jeans and T-shirt she wore. She suddenly seemed too small and fragile to have withstood hardship or suffered adversity. And with the wealth her mother had, it would seem there was no reason she should have. But Reese knew money and suffering weren't mutually exclusive. You could have an abundance of one and still not find a way to escape the other.

Under his brief scrutiny her shoulders stiffened and her jaw tightened another notch.

After all the shouting, her quiet voice took him off guard. "Listen, I'm sorry you came all this way, that you risked . . . anything. But as I told the gentlemen who came by yesterday, I'm not leaving. I can't." The last was added on a somewhat defensive note, her sudden blink telling him she hadn't planned on saying it out loud.

"Won't," he countered. "Not the same thing."

"It doesn't matter. The result is the same. I'd suggest you find whatever vehicle you drove here in and leave quickly. I have to finish securing the house."

He saw her gaze dart nervously over his shoulder to the door and spacious yard beyond. The area surrounding her small house was more of a compound. Reese knew she rehabilitated marine and local wildlife in conjunction with several refuges in the area. But other than the alligator, he hadn't seen any signs of other animals. The assorted pens and cages near the rear building appeared empty.

So what was keeping her here? He'd pegged her a survivor. Survivors didn't put their lives on the line without a damn good reason. And as far as he could tell, there wasn't one in sight. He gave a mental shrug. He didn't care, because it didn't matter. She was leaving now. And despite how angry it made her, he doubted she'd hold that grudge when she realized he'd saved her life.

And yet something about her compelled him to try to understand. Not bothering to examine the urge, he simply asked her, "Why?"

"Because if I want a scarecrow's chance in hell of living through this, I'm going to need to do a bit more work."

"I meant, why aren't you going? All the securing in the world won't keep this place from going up like Dorothy's house on its way to Oz. Only I doubt you'll be so lucky."

"Why do you care?" She held up her hand. "Never mind, stupid question. You obviously take your job as part of the evacuation effort very seriously. I respect what you're trying to do here." She gestured around her, but Reese knew she meant the entire evacuation zone that encompassed the lower half of Florida's gulf coastline. "But I think your time would be more wisely spent helping those people who want to be rescued."

Her voice had taken on a gentle, soothing quality. He imagined wounded animals responded very well to it. Lucky for him he was a man and immune to such precarious things as a woman's soft voice.

"Time's up." He took her arm, though a bit more gently this time, grabbing a box of trash bags off her kitchen table as he moved toward the office he could see through the open door behind her. Once inside, he let her go, blocking the door with his body, then pulled a couple of bags free. "Here. Just the most important things. I'll be back in five minutes."

He ducked out the door, grabbing a ladder-back chair from beside the table behind him and shoving it under the doorknob. He'd barely gotten it tightly wedged when she began jiggling it.

"Hey! You can't do this! Let me out of here!" She banged on the heavy wooden door.

"You're wasting time," he called back, then grabbed a few more bags and went in search of her room.

A loud thwack behind him indicated she'd kicked the door. The following string of curse words trailed him up the stairs.

Where in the hell had she learned to swear like that?

His grimace faded. What replaced it couldn't be called a smile. Reese Braedon never smiled.

But he had to admit he wasn't bored anymore.

Bored. It was disconcerting to realize that until that moment, he hadn't been able to put his finger on what his problem had been of late. It had been almost a year since he'd thrown in the federal towel and opened up a private security agency with Cole Sinclair, another agent he'd occasionally worked with in his past life.

Bored. Eighteen months ago, he'd craved boredom like a man who'd spent far too many years living on the edge of his wits. Like the man he was. Had been. Private security allowed him the luxury of picking his own jobs. And more importantly, being his own boss. He'd never again find himself in the position of having to answer to someone else, particularly when people's lives were on the line.

Reese shoved aside the dark memories of his past. He elbowed his way into the first room at the top of the stairs. The steel shutters made the room dark, so he flipped the light switch. It was a bedroom, but it wasn't hers. Too neat and tidy, with an air of expectancy, like it was just waiting for an aunt or a cousin to drop in for a brief stay.

But not a mother, he thought with a wry twist of his lips. Without giving any details, Regina Ravensworth had made it very clear that she and her daughter were not close. In fact, the one promise she'd wrung from him was that he not tell Jillian why he'd been hired—or that he'd been hired at all.

He'd agreed to the condition, knowing Jillian would probably assume he was part of the evacuation effort. Which he had been earlier that week down in the Keys, where he and Sinclair lived and headquartered their business.

However, at this point, he didn't see where keeping her mother's role out of it had made the job a whole helluva lot easier.

He flipped off the guest room light and moved down the hall. One bathroom, another guest room, one linen closet. He paused long enough to grab a few sheets, some towels, and a blanket, then moved to the next door . . . And stopped cold on the threshold.

This was her room.

It wasn't just the large double bed covered with the jumble of lemon-yellow sheets that gave it away. He stepped inside, feeling strangely like the intruder he was. He never gave his methods much thought, just doing what had to be done in the most efficient manner possible to obtain his goal. And this was far from the first time he'd found himself in the bedroom of a woman he'd just met. Of course, he'd usually been invited. He shrugged off the odd feeling and looked around.

The room wasn't feminine. Bare hardwood floors, a bed, one nightstand, and a wooden dresser. The only adornment was a watercolor of a marsh scene hanging over the dresser and a wooden lamp carved in the shape of a leaping dolphin on the nightstand. No pictures or well-thumbed paperbacks lay on the nightstand, no watches or jewelry littered the scarred surface of the dresser.

Picturing her small plain features, slim boyish

body clad in a shapeless T-shirt and jeans and her job working with animals, he supposed it shouldn't surprise him that there weren't the requisite bottles, tubes, and pots of makeup and cologne cluttering every available surface.

Although there was a faint fresh scent in the air, sort of woodsy. Odd for a woman, he thought, then admitted that it somehow suited her. A disconcerting notion considering he barely knew her. Didn't want to know her. She was just another job. So what if she intrigued him? She was a puzzle he didn't have time to solve. The problem, he acknowledged with a frown, was getting rid of the inclination.

It occurred to him with a start that he was wasting precious time, standing there literally sniffing around. He bent down and grabbed two pairs of worn sneakers from the floor by the door and dumped them into the trash bag, then turned back to the dresser opposite her bed.

He tugged at the top drawer but it held tight, probably warped from the constant humidity. He yanked harder. The drawer sprang open past its tracks, upending her underwear in a heap on the floor.

"God—" Reese bit off the curse, set the drawer down and knelt, careful to favor his thigh. He hadn't given a thought to her lingerie—she was hardly the type to inspire heated fantasies—but the basic white cotton bras and undies spilling from his hands didn't provide any surprises.

He stuffed a handful of each, along with some white crew socks in the bag. He reached for the second drawer and pulled out several pairs of faded blue jeans. Shorts, T-shirts, and a few old sweat-shirts followed as he searched the other drawers.

He scooped up the remaining pile of underwear and dumped it back in the warped drawer. The sound of something hard and metallic stilled his actions for a moment, then he shoved a hand into the jumble and rooted around until his fingers closed over what felt like a picture frame.

He pulled out the small, gilt-edged frame and flipped it over. It was a photo of a man seated next to a woman with a small child in her lap. Judging by the not-quite-true colors and clothing, the photo had been taken some time ago.

He recognized the woman immediately as Regina Ravensworth, although from what he knew of her background, he doubted that had been her last name back then. Reese wasn't surprised to see she'd been even more stunning as a young woman. She was leaning against the shoulder of a big, brawny, blond man who was looking off to his left, away from Regina and the child she held in her lap. Regina's expression was plainly adoring, almost pain-fully so.

Reese's gaze dropped to the child cradled loosely in her lap. She looked about three or four and had a mop of dark curls. Jillian, he presumed. What kept his attention riveted to the photo was the expression on the child's face. Her small head was tilted back, and she was staring up at her mother. The unconditional love stamped on her tiny features wasn't surprising. Nor was it what made Reese's heart feel strangely tight. It was the intense yearning in those bright gray eyes. Innocently unconcealed, unafraid of possible discovery, as only the young could afford to risk.

What in the world would make a young girl look at her own mother that way? And if Regina had looked down in the instant after the photo was snapped, would Jillian have received reassurance that she, too, was adored? Or would she receive rejection?

Or worse yet, would she encounter the same thing Reese had repeatedly found as a small boy, before he'd learned not to go looking anymore. Would she look up into the eyes of a mother who wouldn't recognize the need was there at all?

The wind snapped a branch against the side of the house, bringing Reese sharply, thankfully, back to the present. He started to shove the photo back into the drawer, then changed his mind. Reaching into the bag, he pulled out one of her sweatshirts and carefully bundled the old frame before tucking it in with the rest of her clothes.

Not wanting to put a reason to his motives, he stood, the ache in his thigh a welcome piece of reality to hang on to. He jimmied the drawer back into place and moved to the small bathroom. He quickly emptied the contents of her medicine chest into another bag and knotted it.

It wasn't until he turned back to face her bedroom that it hit him. The reason he'd frozen on the doorstep when he'd first stepped into her room, the reason he'd felt so odd as he'd stood there, cataloguing her personal effects, or more precisely, the lack thereof.

The reason it all felt so strange was because it was familiar. Very familiar. Too familiar.

Her bedroom was distant, no connections to anyone here, nothing tying her to past memories, past dreams, fulfilled or otherwise. Except an old photo hidden away in a dresser drawer.

Reese pictured the small, isolated bungalow he lived in on Vaca Key. Every room in that house looked amazingly just like this one. Full of furniture, empty of soul.

Which suited him perfectly. So perfectly he'd never even noticed anything lacking.

Until now, a tiny voice whispered inside his brain.

He ruthlessly snuffed it out. Irritated, and not at all happy about the reasons for it, Reese hefted the two bags toward the hall.

He had to turn sideways to fit the bags and himself through the narrow doorway, then was forced to balance the whole pile on one knee so he could reach back inside to flip the switch. Unfortunately, he forgot about his thigh injury and he wobbled precariously for a split second.

A half second later, the hard muzzle of a gun—his if he wasn't mistaken—pressed into his lower back.

"What in the bloody hell are you—?"

"Freeze!"

TWO

Reese hung his head. "Christ almighty." He continued swearing under his breath as he dropped the bags of clothes and slowly raised his hands. This would be funny if it weren't so damn frustrating. First the alligator. Now he was being held at gunpoint with his own gun, by the woman whose life he was trying to save. Sinclair would laugh his ass off if he ever found out. Which Reese would make damn sure he never did.

No job was worth this sort of aggravation. Reese considered telling her he knew a dozen ways to easily disarm her, most of them painful, then discarded that idea as too time-consuming. He had to admit it though, she had pluck.

He hated pluck.

"I want you to put your hands on your head and walk slowly to the stairs. Then I want you to go down them and straight out the back door and off my property."

He didn't have time for this. Correction. *They* didn't have time for this. "You've been watching too many cop shows." As he said this, he twisted suddenly and brought his bad leg up, knee bent, knocking the gun from her hand, allowing him to grab her arms and pin her to the wall across the narrow hallway.

He pressed against her narrow frame, hot daggers needling his wound where it had—of course—come into direct contact with the butt of his gun. If it wasn't for the humiliation factor of the explanation he'd have to give, he'd demand Mrs. Ravensworth pay him double time for this one.

"Don't hurt me," she said quietly, her soft voice neither pleading nor demanding.

"Don't tempt me," Reese shot back, but he relaxed his hold and moved back a fraction of an inch, his frustration more self-directed than aimed at her. Again his gaze tangled with hers. Wide gray eyes, looking enormous in her small face, stared warily back at him. Her short hair was plastered to her head, her.T-shirt wet and clinging . . .

Wait a minute. She was soaked.

"How did you get out?"

"Climbed through the office window onto the porch. I hadn't gotten that one covered yet."

"It's started to rain," he said, more to himself. "Ivan's closing in. We've got to get outta here."

Holding one wrist, he bent down, pulling her

awkwardly with him, and grabbed his gun. He thrust one bag at her, which she grasped automatically, then scooped up the other one. "Did you pack the one I gave you?"

"No, because—"

He was already pulling her toward the stairs. "Tough luck then, your time's run out."

"But—"

He heaved a sigh, silently cursing his sore thigh and her in no particular order. "No buts. What is it you Yanks say? No more Mr. Nice Guy."

She tugged hard but to no avail. "You call this nice?"

He glared at her over his shoulder. "I call this keeping you alive." He stalked to the back door. "No time for utilities. Probably won't be anything left anyway."

"I'm not—"

He turned swiftly and closed the distance between her face and his, stopping her speech as effectively as if he'd covered her mouth with his hand. Or his mouth.

Now where had *that* come from? Reese tore his gaze from her soft lips and pointed it back at her eyes. "You can thank me for saving your life later. Right now, we've got to get back over the bridge, across Sanibel and over that bridge as well. My truck is right outside the front gate."

"Great. Have a safe trip." Her voice was as flat as her eyes.

Her posture made it clear her survival skills

were well honed. Unfortunately she'd pegged *him* as the threat instead of the storm. "Listen, the rain has started, that means—"

"I know what it means. It means that thanks to you, I'm going to get pummeled by the rain while covering up that last window, and I still have other precautions to take."

"To hell with the window! The way the wind is going, we'll be lucky to keep the truck on the road."

"Then go already!" She pushed her face right up into his. "I'm not stopping you."

"You're right." Knowing his thigh would pay dearly for this, he scooped her up and put her over his shoulder. It was either that or give in to the entirely ridiculous urge to kiss her into submission. He felt her hands grab at the back of his jacket and lift it up, so he quickly shifted his gun to the front of his jeans.

He headed out the back door with both trash bags in one hand, her thighs clamped in the other. And he refused to even think about that tight little piece of her anatomy bouncing next to his ear. The heightened wind and pelting rain was no match for the curses she was hurling at him. He heard every one of them. Quiet and reserved, huh? Regina had apparently been estranged from her daughter for a very long time.

While half of his mind worked to ignore Jillian's protests and the feel of supple muscle flexing under his hands as she thrashed, the other half kept a lookout for Cleo. The driving rain made scanning the grounds difficult, but he saw no sign of the creature. He only hoped Cleo's vision was as impaired as his.

The skies had darkened considerably, not a good sign. The hurricane warning had been posted early that morning and the report he'd heard right before he'd left his truck predicted they had roughly ten hours before it ripped up the lower western coastline. The way things looked now, they'd be lucky to get half that.

He had to bend low to force himself forward, covering little ground with each staggering step. He reached the gate in the high wire mesh fence that lined her property. Shoving with one shoulder, he was able to get it open wide enough to squeeze through, the wind slamming it shut behind him.

Pressing the bags between his hip and the side of his black pickup truck, he opened the driver's door, tossed the bags in the storage area behind the seat then bent down to deposit her on the bench seat. He grunted at the pain the motion caused, gritting his teeth when her booted toe caught him square in the center of the gash.

"Slide over."

His answer was a steely-eyed glare. He climbed in and forced her to move or be sat on. She scrambled over the gear shift, and he grabbed at the rear belt loop of her jeans just as her hand hit the passenger side door handle.

He pulled her back and reached across her,

yanking the seat belt across her lap with a bit more force than necessary. Then he turned to her so their faces almost touched. "Do I have to tie you to the dashboard?"

His question met with stony silence.

"Fine, have it your way." He reached behind him and grappled around until he found a length of rope.

"Don't even think about it," she warned.

"And let you jump out the minute I start the truck?" He grabbed at her hands, securing them with the white cord then leaning across her to loop it through the large steering wheel. He left enough slack so he could turn the wheel without tangling the rope.

He started the truck, vowing not to look at her, even briefly, until they were off the island. This wasn't at all how he'd planned this, but dammit, it wasn't like he was willingly trying to hurt her. So there was no reason why he should feel the least bit guilty. Guilt was an emotion he'd long ago decided was a luxury he couldn't afford. Along with trust, faith, love, and a few other human frailties that could get a man killed.

Shoving the gearshift into reverse, he propped one arm on the seat and turned to look over his shoulder as he backed out. His gaze came to a reluctant halt when it met hers.

"Why are you forcing me to do this? I don't want to go."

If she'd pleaded with him, or cried or begged

him, he would have been able to ignore her. But her solemn voice, combined with the defeat and pain etched so eloquently in her soft gray eyes gave him pause. Her look as good as said he was all but ripping her life to shreds. That she'd managed to survive all her battles, only to have him step in and toss another one at her feet. No matter the strength of her fight, that trace of what he'd seen earlier in her eyes told him she simply couldn't handle another loss.

Couldn't she see that was what he was trying to avoid?

"Because it's my job to make sure you're safe," he answered, his voice for once devoid of the anger and frustration he'd aimed at her since she'd nailed him to the ground in a flying tackle.

"Even if it's not what I want?"

He didn't have an answer for that. He stared at her for a long moment, for the first time wondering if he was doing the right thing. Part of him wanted to argue with her that he was saving her life. But an even stronger urge prodded him to pull her into his lap and hold her, tell her he was sorry.

But he wasn't sorry he was about to save her life. He might have convinced himself she was just a job, but somewhere between accepting Regina's offer and sitting here in the cab of his truck with her daughter, he'd gone from *wanting* to save Jillian's life because he was being paid to, to *needing* to save her life because . . . Because he didn't want her to get hurt.

Reese abruptly turned his attention to the road behind him, wishing it was as simple as that. Wishing his mind weren't as fogged as the rear window.

It took all his skills to maneuver the truck toward the single bridge connecting them with Sanibel Island. Jillian hadn't said a word since they'd backed away from the compound. He'd half expected her to be sobbing by now, but several quick glances told him that she had turned her head to her window, her gaze glued to the large rearview mirror just beyond it and the increasing distance he was putting between her and the house.

"Maybe the brunt of the hurricane will miss it," he said after a moment, then felt foolish for trying to comfort her when she didn't answer.

He made the last turn, his attention drawn to his right and a downed tree that almost blocked their path.

"I hope you're right," she said suddenly.

"Why?" he asked, then turned to follow her gaze.

Again, she didn't answer. She didn't have to.

Half of the bridge was gone.

Twisted planks and a crumble of cement were all that remained of their only link to Sanibel and the rest of Florida.

Two things struck Jillian Bonner almost simultaneously. The first was a gut-level response to the scene in front of her, visual proof of the risk she'd taken in deciding to stay. Although it hadn't really been a choice as far as she was concerned. She'd made a commitment to Cleo.

The second, and almost more overwhelming realization was that she was stuck with this surly Neanderthal for the duration of the storm. Her gaze shifted to the large blond man scowling next to her.

For the first time she wished she'd evacuated with the other locals.

"Well," she said, looking back to the destruction in front of her. "At least that takes care of one thing."

Out of the corner of her eye, she saw him hang his head, then shake it slowly, like a man who'd been pushed beyond the point of endurance. All things considered, she shouldn't want to smile. There was nothing remotely amusing about being ordered around, tossed over a shoulder, then tied to a steering wheel. But she had the oddest feeling that he wasn't often thrown for a loop. And the idea that she had just hog-tied him with one pricked her admittedly off-the-wall sense of humor.

"And what in the hell might that be?" he asked finally, resting his brawny forearms on the large steering wheel and turning to face her.

Her desire to smile became a distant memory. The serene smile that did cross her face was a calculated one. Calculated to cinch that loop just a bit tighter. Visualizing it around his neck, she said, "Now I won't have to waste my valuable time reporting you to the authorities for kidnapping."

"Attempted kidnapping," he responded, not lifting so much as an eyebrow hair at her declaration.

Determined to match his steady, unaffected gaze, she said, "Exactly my point. Now would you please turn this four-wheel-drive prison around? I'd like at least to be indoors before Ivan pays a visit." She shifted facing front and folded her hands calmly in her lap, at least as best she could considering she was still in bondage.

It took considerable concentration to control the nerves that made her stomach quake and threatened to start a noticeable trembling in her arms and legs. *You've faced down more ornery creatures than this one*, she reminded herself. Both human and reptile.

And yet the feel of his eyes on her was one of the most unnerving sensations she'd ever felt. She chalked it up to the probable wild shifts in the barometric pressure.

A loud crack made her jump and spin around. A huge limb from an oak tree beside the road had just snapped off like a dry twig. She spun back around to face him. "Can we get out of here? Now? Please?"

"Don't get those nice cotton undies in a twist," he shot back, then turned to the road as he threw the gearshift in reverse.

He's been through my underwear drawer?

So preoccupied by that mental picture, it didn't occur to Jillian until they'd reached the gated entrance to her compound that he hadn't jumped at the sudden noise from the breaking tree limb.

Didn't anything faze this guy?

She watched him give the grounds a surreptitious once-over. A smile threatened again. She knew one thing.

Cleo.

"Give me your wrist."

She'd noticed his accent earlier, but for some reason it just now truly caught her attention. Probably because he wasn't yelling at her. She held up her bound hand, and he made short work of the knots. "Thanks ever so much," she said, mocking his accent by injecting as much dripping sarcasm into the words as possible.

"It's not like you're going anywhere," he muttered.

Before she could respond, he reached behind the seat and heaved one of the trash bags into her lap. "You take this and I'll take croc watch."

"American alligator," she corrected as she grabbed the knotted plastic. "And as long as you don't get between her and her egg mound, she won't bother you."

His answer was a grunt just before he slid out of the truck. Jillian climbed out quickly and toted the bag toward the gate. Any part of her that hadn't been soaked before became instantly so now. The screaming wind pushed her into a stumbled run. They both reached for the gate at the same time. Slammed into it actually.

"Move back and I'll open it!" he yelled over the wind.

It was a measure of how much the gales had increased that he was standing two inches from her and she'd read his lips more than heard the words.

"Fine!" she yelled back. She saw him reach for the gun at his waist. "No guns!" He glared at her as they shoved their way through the gate, prompting a dry smile. "Don't worry, I'll protect you!"

His scowl deepened, proving he was as good at reading lips as she was.

As best she could in the darkening gloom, Jillian scanned the grounds near the small pond Cleo had staked out shortly after her arrival. She could just barely make out the dark form of the alligator hovering over the huge pile of leaves, twigs, and debris she'd laboriously scraped into a three-foot-high pile to incubate her eggs.

Another gust buffeted her against the large man at her side, pulling her thoughts from Cleo and her nestlings to more immediate problems. Sending a silent prayer—one of many—Cleo's way, she hunched down and pushed toward the enclosed back porch.

The rain was being driven by the wind into horizontal slashes making it difficult to do much more than squint. Jillian lunged for the screened door to the back porch. A gust caught her just as she was about to push through, jerking her back until she tottered precariously on the top step. A sudden shove sent her snapping forward.

The trash bag went flying, with her landing in an ignominious heap on top of it a second later. She rolled to her left, fearing she'd be crushed if he fell on top of her, then became quickly tangled in the contents of the bag which had split open on impact.

A loud thud echoed next to her in the space she'd narrowly vacated. Swearing followed, his accent thickening to the point of making him almost impossible to understand. She was too busy wrestling with whatever it was she'd become entangled in to care.

Suddenly, a large tan hand reached for her. She leaned away automatically, but he just pulled at whatever had tangled on her head, freeing it with a short snap.

"Here," he said, handing it to her. "Though I don't see why you bother," he muttered.

A hot flush crept over her entire body as she took the bra he'd so gallantly offered. She told herself it was anger not humiliation that burned her skin, that she'd long ago come to terms with her underendowed figure. Besides which, the very last thing she wanted from him was *that* sort of attention. She was grateful he'd made his feelings on the subject clear. Grateful and relieved.

And certainly not surprised.

"Thank you," she said in the ultrapolite tone

she'd been schooled in during her younger years. She hadn't needed that particular skill in ages, but had to admit it came in handy just now. With the same studied dignity, she tucked the small white cotton bra under her arm and turned away to scoop up the rest of her belongings, already half-soaked by the rain slashing through the screened windows.

For several long moments she sensed him looking at her as she wadded up the pile of clothing. "Didn't your mother teach you it's not nice to stare?" she muttered. He responded with the same stony expression she was rapidly coming to think was his only alternative to scowling. The least he could do was help, she thought as she struggled to her feet, her own wet clothes making her motions awkward. "I thought you Brits were brought up with impeccable manners."

"I'm Australian."

She shot him a look. "Well, that explains it then."

His blue eyes widened.

And what incredible eyes they were, she thought, distracted momentarily as she stared back at him. Clear and bright. And hard. As if all the soul had been leeched out.

She wondered what had happened to him to make his eyes so empty. She wasted another second imagining what a decent smile would do to them, then snorted at the folly.

Considering his temperament, she doubted

she'd ever find out. Nor should she want to, she reminded herself.

Jerking her gaze from his, she stepped forward and stumbled. He reacted instantly, steadying her with a firm grip. His hands felt huge on her. One hand wrapped well around her hip, his palm on her jutting hipbone, his fingers digging into the soft flesh of her . . .

She pulled away, wobbled, then straightened. "Thanks," she said, chalking up the breathless quality of her voice to her struggle and not the feel of his hands on her backside.

"We'd better get this stuff inside. I still have one window to cover and—"

"Jillian." His even voice cut her off.

He had the oddest expression on his face. Almost as if he were in pain of some kind. The idea bothered her more than she cared to admit. After all, he'd toted her around like a rolled-up carpet for goodness sake. She should be happy to see him suffer.

But it wasn't in her to create suffering. She'd been on the receiving end enough for one lifetime. Maybe two. Now she worked long hours to alleviate pain. And doubly hard to avoid it herself.

Besides, she told herself, determined not to soften toward him even the tiniest bit, he was far too big for a simple fall on the porch to hurt him. Too hardheaded to let it bother him if by some miracle it had. She turned back to her task, away from those clear eyes that did strange things to her when he wasn't bullying her or shouting orders.

"Don't just sit there," she said shortly, "the least you can do after dragging me through the rain is to help. After all, it's your hide on the line too."

"If you'd come with me when I'd asked, that wouldn't be the case," he reminded her.

She pushed the kitchen door open and dumped the heap of clothes on the counter. Turning back, she found him still sitting on her porch, staring at her. The sight of his big brawny body sitting casually amongst her underwear should have been amusing. Instead it twisted something inside her chest. The image of that same big body, all tanned muscles and streaked blond hair, tangled up in lemon-yellow sheets—her lemon-yellow sheets— tumbled through her mind before she could shut it out.

"I didn't ask to be rescued," she said tightly. "That was your idea. But now that you're here, you can turn off the electricity." She turned for the door. "The fuse box is in the pantry off the kitchen."

Not giving him time to answer, she headed to the front hall to get her slicker, mentally shutting off electricity of an entirely different—but just as dangerous—sort.

It occurred to her that putting on her rain gear now was somewhat pointless, but she shoved her arms into the sleeves anyway. The wind made the rain needle-sharp and this would give her at least a measure of protection.

"I'll put the window covers on."

Jillian whirled around to find Reese standing just behind her. He was also soaked, but somehow his sodden khaki vest jacket, black T-shirt, and faded jeans made him seem that much bigger, that much more masculine. Her pulse leapt into double time along with her heart. She half expected the air around him to crackle and hiss.

"No . . . I mean, thanks, but getting them into the track is tricky."

The corners of his mouth twisted. Sardonic grin or grimace. It was hard to tell with him. The expression never seemed to reach those soulless eyes.

"I think I can handle it. Where are the metal sheets?"

Guessing from his earlier tenacity that arguing would only waste valuable time, she sighed and answered him. "Under the back porch."

"Flashlight?"

"In a cardboard box on the counter in the kitchen. There's also propane and battery-operated lanterns, extra batteries, and some small propane tanks."

He nodded and headed down the hall.

"Do you want a slicker or something?" she called after him, unable to look away from the way his wet vest showcased the difference in width between his broad shoulders and narrow waist.

"Hardly any need at this point." He paused in

the kitchen, and she could hear him rummaging through the boxes as she peeled her raincoat off and hung it up.

He looked up as she entered the kitchen. "Here's the battery lantern. Turn it on before you shut off the power."

She took it from him, careful not to brush her fingers against his, feeling foolish when the metal handle didn't spark under her fingertips. His instructions annoyed her and she was tempted to tell him she wasn't an idiot, but considering her reaction to him just now, she didn't want to chance having him argue that point.

Expecting—mentally urging—him to leave, she bent her head to check the lantern out. When he remained standing in front of her, she reluctantly lifted her gaze to his.

In the silent moment that followed, neither moved or spoke. The escalating noise of the storm began to make her heart pound again. At least, that's what she told herself.

"We should shut off the water," he said finally. "Fill the tubs and sinks with water first, though."

"Done. I also have bleach on hand in case the water supply is contaminated and several coolers full of bottled water. I've prepared for storms before, Mr.—" She stopped abruptly as it occurred to her that during all the tumult she'd never even learned his name.

"Braedon. Reese."

He rattled it off in a short, flat cadence that made her wonder if he was about to follow with rank and serial number. "Well, Mr. Braedon, I've lived here—"

"Seeing as how I've been intimate with your underwear, I think you can call me Reese."

She refused to blush. He'd made it more than clear he found her underwear more practical than intimate. Which, of course, was precisely why she'd purchased it. She had no need for flimsy silk underthings that would fall apart at the first hint of usage. Nope. No use at all.

"Maybe you'd better get outside before it gets worse."

He stared at her for another silent moment, then turned and went out the back door. Ridiculously, she felt a hollowness in the pit of her stomach. His brief, but thorough appraisal had made it clear that she'd come up as lacking in her choice of underthings. Any electricity she'd felt had been one-sided. The loud thwack of the screen door slamming against its frame startled her from her thoughts.

It had been a long time since she'd had the slightest urge to measure herself on the surface scale of beauty. Physical perfection, and how one could use it to insure personal wealth and security, was her mother's obsession, not hers. And goodness knows Regina had tallied up her daughter's shortcomings often enough to compensate for both of them.

Frowning, she shoved all thoughts of her mother to their usual far corner of her mind, then tucked her unusual reaction to Reese Braedon in another dark soon-to-be-forgotten corner and turned to the task of securing the rest of the house.

THREE

Jillian reentered the kitchen and noticed the trash bag sitting on the floor. Reese must have picked up her clothes earlier. She hadn't noticed. She'd been too preoccupied . . .

Just then the back door blew open with a bang. Reese's huge frame filled the doorway, a stark figure silhouetted by the black skies behind him. She was immediately drawn to his face. His jaw was clenched so tightly, it made his cheekbones stand out in sharp relief, the light in his eyes was wild, almost feral. What in the hell was wrong with him?

He gripped the doorframe with both hands, as if in fear he'd be sucked back out into the storm. She saw his mouth move, but the noise outside was so loud, she couldn't hear herself think much less what he was saying. More afraid of him now than when he'd held her against the wall in the upstairs hallway, she knew her greater concern had to be getting him out of the open doorway before the door blew off its hinges. Besides, after the way he'd fought to get her safely off the island, she doubted he meant her any harm now.

She ran to him and grabbed his arm. "Get inside!"

He didn't answer, but when she tugged, his grip on the frame just tightened. Jillian looked up at him so he could read her lips. "Move!"

"Bloody . . . I can't!" His accent had thickened to a growl.

"What?" His words sunk in. "Why?"

As an answer, he slumped against one side of the door and would have lost his balance entirely if she hadn't shifted quickly to wedge herself between him and the doorframe. As it was he almost squashed her as she struggled to keep him upright. "You're hurt!" She didn't know where or how, but it was obvious he wasn't in great shape.

He bent his head so his mouth was closer to her ear. "Move outta . . . the way. Gotta . . . close . . . the door."

She wrapped her arm around his waist. It was like hugging a big tree. "Let go!" she yelled, unable to look up so he could see her lips move. Her head just reached his shoulder.

Bracing her legs for his weight, she reached up for the hand still gripping the door, intending to pull it down around her shoulder. It was then she felt the sticky warmth against her hip. Looking down she saw the cause. He had a long slash down the outside of his thigh which had bled through his jeans and soaked into hers. She looked up to say something, but he chose that moment to let his good knee buckle, sending them staggering into the kitchen and half across the table.

Reese fell face and chest forward onto the table with a loud groan. Jillian was slung into the chairs, but managed to catch hold of one before she tumbled to the floor. She scrambled up and ran to close the door, shoving hard against the fierce gusts shoving back. As soon as it clicked, she slammed the dead bolt across and raced back to Reese who was hugging the table, probably to keep from sliding into a heap on the floor.

She grabbed a chair and turned it at an angle. "Reese?"

He grunted.

"Can you roll to your right? I'll hold the chair and you can slide into it and leave your leg straight in front of you."

His answer was to shift his hands slowly around the table as he gradually did what she'd asked. Once he'd slid into the chair, he let his head drop back for a moment, his eyes tightly shut.

She leaned over him. "Reese?"

He opened one eye.

"What happened to your leg?"

"Alligator."

"*What?*" It was the last thing she'd expected, and her voice rose several octaves in surprise. "Cleo's halfway across the compound. Even in the storm, it wouldn't make any sense for her to charge you—"

"Earlier. Caught me off guard. Snagged my thigh. Just before you tackled me."

Jillian flashed back to the first time she'd seen him. Crouching in front of Cleo with a gun pointed down her throat. Was that why he'd pulled a gun on her? She'd gotten a hold of him?

"You mean you've been running around in this storm, dragging half my clothes and me over your shoulder with a huge gash in your thigh?"

He opened his other eye. "Wasn't my idea."

"But—"

He raised his hand to forestall her next question. "It wasn't that bad." He shifted slightly, winced, waited a moment, then went on. "Until the metal sheet slipped and the corner caught it."

She gasped. "Ouch!" The reaction was automatic. "It's a miracle you made it back to the porch."

He shook his head. "The miracle is that I got the bloody thing on." He spoke through gritted teeth. "If you have anything to secure that door, do it now before the wind blows it in."

Jillian spun to the door, her eyes widening at the way it shuddered against its hinges as the storm pounded it even with the screened-in porch providing some protection.

She thought she'd have more time. Earlier, just before she'd gone outside to check on Cleo—only to find Reese holding the alligator at gunpoint—

she'd heard the radio update stating they'd have at least ten hours. They'd predicted wrong.

Suddenly, everything overwhelmed her. The reality of the storm, Cleo facing it alone as she protected her eggs, and now Reese's nasty wound. They all needed her attention.

Grabbing a battery lantern, she hurried to her office where she'd stashed the metal bars that slipped into brackets across the back door, counting her blessings that she'd spent the money to install the heavy-duty storm safeguards after witnessing the devastation of Hurricane Andrew.

Shutting out the instant-replay images the media had been showing at all hours ever since Hurricane Ivan was determined to be heading this way, she nonetheless cast an anxious look at the now-shuttered window. She'd hoped to do one last check on Cleo and had left her office window for last because it provided a direct view of the egg mound and the pond. The quick check she'd made just before Reese dragged her to the house would have to suffice. For now, Cleo was on her own.

She tugged the bars from her office and shoved them into the slots. After the last one slid into place, she leaned on the door and took a deep breath. The house was now as protected as it was going to get.

Which left Reese.

She turned back to face him. He'd shifted enough to line his leg up with the chair opposite him and looked as if he was about to lift it.

"Don't!" She moved quickly to his side. "You could aggravate the wound."

"Aggravate? I'd say it's pretty p.o.'d already." He winced, then clenched his jaw as he reached forward for his calf.

"I'll do it." But he batted her hands away and with a loud groan, pulled his leg up and rested it on the seat of the chair in front of him. She quickly moved another one under his foot so his whole leg was supported.

"And you think I'm stubborn."

"I know you're stubborn," he said as he leaned over to inspect the wound. "Bring the lantern closer."

Swearing under her breath, she grabbed a second battery lantern from the box and carried them both to the table. "Move back so I can look."

"It's not that bad," he pronounced, still bent over, pulling at the torn fabric. "The impact just sort of jolted me is all. I'll be fine." When she didn't say anything, he looked up at her. "Got some thread and a needle?"

"You going to do that for yourself too?"

"You ever sewn up a man?"

Something in his expression made her wonder what he would answer if she'd been the one asking. "Birds, small mammals, and the occasional reptile," she answered, determined not to be curious about Reese Braedon. "Don't worry, I won't notice the difference."

"Very funny."

Taking that comment for his assent, Jillian picked up one lantern. "I'll be right back."

After collecting supplies from the boxes she'd packed and stored in the coverted storage closet the day before, she hurried back to the kitchen.

Scrubbing her hands over the empty side of her double sink with some of the bottled water, she pulled on surgical gloves, then laid a sterile cloth on the table and quickly organized her supplies so she could easily reach them. "I'll need you to hold the lantern up so I can see. If you feel the least bit woozy, tell me immediately so I can stop. Warn me if you have to move."

She knelt on the floor beside him and plucked at the ragged edges of his jeans. The tear in the fabric was about five inches long. Peeling it back, she allowed a small sigh of relief as she saw that the wound was shorter by about two inches. Still, it looked deep and definitely needed cleaning. And stitching.

She reached up for the scissors but he beat her to them.

"I'm not helpless here. Tell me what you want and I'll hand it to you."

"I *want* you to follow directions."

"You're one to talk about following directions."

The man was aggravation personified. So why did she have the sudden, strange urge to smile? Ignoring the possibility that she was actually enjoying their verbal sparring, Jillian avoided looking directly at him as she took the scissors, then deftly slit the denim, elongating the tear.

"Be careful, Doc, those are my only pants."

She looked up at him, not bothering to hide her smile. "That's a shame, because I have to cut them off to get the wound cleansed properly." She bent back to her task. "And I'm not a doctor."

"You're not cutting off my—What did you say?"

She glanced back up, her tone and expression serious. "I'm not a doctor. I'm a wildlife rehabilitator with some basic medical skills." When he didn't immediately grab the scissors away from her, she went back to work, then paused to look up at him again before cutting further. "Would you rather take them off?"

Jillian prayed he'd say no. Somehow she was certain she'd only embarrass herself more with this man if she was forced to kneel over his bare thigh with only his underwear as a barrier between her eyes and his . . . She gulped. She doubted plain white cotton would look utilitarian on him. And there was always the chance he didn't wear any. Dear Lord.

"Just don't cut them off altogether." His voice was rough, but not angry like she'd become accustomed to.

Had he seen something of her thoughts in her eyes? She bent her head and went back to work on his jeans. No, she thought as she slit the fabric crossways at the top and bottom of the tear. If he

•

had, surely he wouldn't have passed on the chance to torment her with it.

Not as relieved as she'd like to be, Jillian folded back the flaps and cleansed the area around the wound as best she could. After replacing the cap on the antiseptic, she reached for the sealed syringe packet and small vial of anesthetic.

"What's that?"

"It's to numb the skin."

"I'd rather have a drink."

Something in his tone was too flat, too gruff. Even for Reese. She looked up at him, careful to keep her expression one of solemn understanding. Her voice didn't quite match it. "Afraid of needles, are we? If you want, you can close your eyes. It will only sting a little."

He didn't respond right away. Something about the way he set his jaw . . . "You aren't going to faint or anything?"

"Not bloody likely."

She quickly shifted her focus back to his wound. The words had been quick, harsh, and certain. So why was she fighting another smile? Other than his understandable wariness of Cleo, she hadn't seen even a trace of vulnerability in him. Quite the opposite.

Jillian absently smoothed the flaps of denim over his thigh, noticing now for some odd reason how hard the muscle was under her fingers. Waist like a tree, thighs like a rock.

And her mind was obviously turning to sap.

With a quick breath for renewed determination, she squared her shoulders and reached for the needle. "Just keep a stiff upper lip and this will be over before you know it."

"You keep rubbing my leg like that and that's not all—Ouch! Dammit, that—Ouch!" He swore under his breath, then said in a steely voice, "You enjoy feeling up your patients before you stab them?"

She carefully laid the syringe down and picked up the antiseptic again. "It might interest you to know that the last critter I worked on had four legs when she came in."

She doused the swab in the clear solution then lifted her head, looking him straight in the eyes. "When I got done, she had only three."

All his sins were being revisited on him in the form of one small, irritating female, Reese decided as he watched Jillian thread a funny-looking curved needle.

And Lord knows, the list wasn't a short one.

"This won't take long." Jillian didn't look up at him as she spoke.

He watched as she poked the needle into his skin. The small numbed area of his thigh wouldn't reduce his effectiveness completely if something were to happen, but nonetheless, he wished she hadn't done it. He'd certainly put up with far worse than being stitched up without benefit of anesthetic.

Reese was used to being in control. Complete, total control. His former career had demanded it at the most basic level, sometimes to the point of making him feel imprisoned by its dictates. His current career reflected the freedom of it, now that complete control was his own choice, both personal and professional.

"How did you come to be a rehabilitator?"

The sudden intrusion of his raspy voice into the continual noise of the storm surprised him as much as it did her. He told himself he'd only asked as a means to take his mind off the storm and the small operation being performed on his thigh. Not out of any real curiosity.

She looked up, studying him warily for a moment, then turned back to tying off neat, precise little black knots in his torn flesh.

"My father was a professor," she said after several seconds passed. "He taught a variety of things, but oceanography was his passion. He died when I was fairly young, but I'd already adopted his love of the ocean. Eventually I became more interested in the creatures that inhabited the water and the surrounding area. I took courses in marine biology, zoology, and several other related subjects. I eventually got involved with a group that specialized in helping birds caught in oil spills. I spent some time up in Alaska after the Valdez spill."

"That's a long way from the Gulf Coast."

If Reese hadn't been studying the narrow lines of her shoulders so closely, he would have missed the slight tightening of the muscles, the stiffening of her spine, even in her curved position. Sore subject? Which part?

Having already decided he wasn't going to allow himself to get involved, he let it drop. It took a moment or two longer for him to erase the resurfacing image of the photo he'd found in her drawer. And yet, as hard as he tried, he couldn't seem to find anything else in the small room to focus on. His gaze remained stubbornly on the small woman kneeling at his feet, tending to him with gentle hands.

"I had a contact with the Fish and Wildlife Department," she said after another silent moment. "When I came back to Florida, I worked for several of the coastal area refuges. I started taking in some injured animals on my own, mostly brought to me by neighbors who knew my background."

She paused as she tied off another knot. "After a while vacationers as well as locals brought injured animals and reptiles they'd found. My success rate of reintroducing them back into their original habitat was good enough that the word spread. I kept adding pens and eventually renovated the old garage to use as a clinic. It wasn't much later that I decided to start a small full-time operation here." She tied off another knot. "Two more and we're done."

Her voice while relating her background had

been matter-of-fact. So why did he get the feeling it had cost her more than she'd ever let on to talk about it so casually? And if so, why hadn't she just told him to mind his own business?

There were a lot of holes in her story. Where the money came from to run her rehab service. Why she'd jumped from marine life to birds and reptiles. Why she'd gone to Alaska. Why she'd come back. Where her feud with her mother figured into all of that.

And why in the hell after all his internal lectures on not getting involved, he still wanted to find out. He'd been hired to keep her from killing herself in the storm, not to dig up dirt on her past.

"Reptiles?" he asked casually, forcing his gaze away from her bent head and back to his surroundings.

He caught her looking up at him out of the corner of his eye, but pretended not to notice. Then she smiled and he found himself turning toward it, naturally, like a plant does to the sun. It . . . warmed him somehow.

Strange. Until that moment, he'd never realized he was cold. Not skin cold, surface cold. Soul cold.

Her soft voice shook him from the disquieting thought.

"I get asked that a lot. No one thinks it's strange to want to save a bird or sea mammal. But tell someone you've worked to save lizards and snakes and they wonder why you bother." Her soft smile turned rueful as she dipped her head back to finishing up her task. "I never could figure the reasoning for that. They're all living things."

"There's a whole side of humanity who barely respects death, Jillian. Much less life."

His quietly spoken words brought her head snapping back up. Gray eyes full of questions he had no intention of answering stared up at him. But the curiosity wasn't the morbid type he found in some women's expressions when he let something of his past slip out. Neither was it the carnal response he'd found some women had when they discovered a man had been intimate with danger. And death.

No. What he saw was far more unsettling. What he saw was . . . understanding.

The wind chose that moment to send something crashing into the side of the house. He didn't so much as flinch. Jillian jumped. All but the hand holding the needle.

She looked away and quickly tied off the last knot, then began bandaging the neatly stitched wound. She had excellent concentration. A skill he readily admired. He imagined it was as crucial at times in her profession as it was in his. Or had been anyway.

Now his life was blessedly quiet, the tension level kept at a minimum since he controlled what sort of work he did. Most times the jobs he took didn't require a tenth of the skills he'd spent all of his adult years honing. It was a facet of his new life he'd expected to enjoy.

After all, he'd more than earned the right not to worry. Not to spend every waking minute wondering if others would die if he made the wrong move, made the wrong decision.

So why was he sitting there, savoring the rush of adrenaline being pumped into his veins? The rush of knowing that, this time, his goal would not be easily accomplished? The rush of knowing that he was going to be challenged?

As Jillian stood and efficiently began gathering up her supplies, Reese found his attention drawn to her again. He openly eyed her dark cropped-off hair, her plain face, devoid of any makeup, her clothes, baggy on her boyish frame even when damp, her callused hands with nails trimmed down almost to the quick.

She wrapped up the small pile she'd made in the sterile cloth, then glanced up, with a look that said she knew he'd been watching her. Assessing her.

"Would you like that drink now? The Novocain will wear off soon." Her voice was even, still soft. But her gray eyes were flat.

"No." He felt the cold emptiness yawning open again deep inside him and wished he could risk the warmth the alcohol would bring. "Make it three aspirin. Extra strength."

She simply nodded and left the kitchen.

Reese stared through the empty doorway for a long moment, wondering why her shift in mood bothered him. Wishing like hell he'd stop feeling like he should apologize.

He turned his attention to his leg. He probed around the bandaged area, then cautiously shifted his leg to the floor. Despite the local, his thigh throbbed, more heated than painful. But he knew that would change shortly and decided it was better to get a handle on his limitations now rather than wait until a crisis forced him to.

Using his shoulder and arm muscles, he levered himself to a stand, then paused, waiting for gravity to do its number on his blood flow. The rush of pain wasn't intolerable. Good. He'd ask Jillian if she could spare a broom handle or something he could use for support. In the meantime, he hopped over to the counter and began taking the lanterns and flashlights out of the box, checking to make sure each worked.

"What in the hell are you doing?"

"What in the hell does it look like I'm doing?" He didn't bother looking up from his task. Nor did he bother to acknowledge the return of that tiny kernel of warmth her voice—despite its tone— seemed to inspire. And he refused to even consider that it felt sort of nice to have someone care about him. On any level.

She crossed the room and took the lantern from his hand. "You should be sitting down with your leg elevated."

He pinned her with a hard gaze, stomping flat his irrational emotional response to her concern. "One thing you should know about me, lady, is that I don't do a lot of things other people think I should." She was close, only inches away. He should just take the lantern back and continue on with what he'd been doing. Even with a leg half out of commission, she would be no match for him.

Yet he didn't move. All he seemed to see was that her eyes weren't lifeless anymore.

"Tell me something I don't know," she shot back, apparently not intimidated in the least by his fierce words.

He half expected her to try to forcibly move him back to the table. After treating him to her best glare, she just huffed a small sigh and grabbed another lantern.

"End of lecture already?" He silently cursed the almost plaintive note that had crept into his voice.

"Yep." She shoved fresh batteries into the base compartment and snapped the cover back on.

"Is this how you treat all your patients?" He had no idea why he was badgering her. After all, it wasn't like he wanted her hanging all over him, dripping with unnecessary concern he didn't need or want.

She turned to rummage in another box on the counter. "No. Though I should thank you for one thing."

He refused to take the bait. But her continued calm, when he felt anything but, gave him the uneasy feeling that he'd wandered too close to the edge of a cliff. He fell back on old defensive tactics in his scramble for safer footing. "Don't bother, I'm sure it was my pleasure."

She lifted hard flat eyes to his. "Yes, there was never any doubt of that."

He sighed heavily. "Would you mind telling me exactly what in the hell we're talking about?" Too late he realized she'd maneuvered him into asking anyway. He scowled, but didn't stop her from answering.

She set the lantern on the counter and faced him squarely. "I've dealt with all sorts of creatures, suffering in a variety of ways. Your attitude merely reinforces my belief that, when it comes to help, human beings are the least appreciative of the lot."

Reese stared at her for a long moment. She looked at him without so much as a blink. He'd lifted his hand halfway to her face before he realized he meant to touch her. He let his hand drop. "Is that why you refused to let me help you? Just being human?" He'd meant the words to be harsh, but his voice sounded damnably gentle.

"I refused to leave with you because I'd made a commitment. I don't make them lightly, and I don't walk away from them just because things get a bit rough."

He lifted his hand again, this time following through on the motion, letting the backs of his knuckles trace softly down the side of her face. Her skin was remarkably smooth and fine. Delicate. Quite the opposite of her personality.

When she didn't smack his hand—or his face—he brought his fingers to rest under her chin. Tilting it up slightly, he was again drawn to the stormy tempest raging quietly inside her.

A dozen questions sprang to his lips, but he asked her nothing. "I won't apologize for trying to save your life. But I am sorry I asked you to compromise your principles." His thumb drifted up to rub softly across her bottom lip. Warm, velvety. Seductive textures so unexpected he was at a loss at how to handle his quick response to them. When he spoke, his voice was barely more than a rough growl. "It's been so long since I've run across a person who had any, I'd stopped expecting to find them."

As the echo of his words faded away, a strange quiet descended between them, a vacuum amidst the howling wind that pounded mercilessly against the house. Reese didn't move his hand, Jillian didn't break their locked gaze. His heart began to pound a heavier rhythm, his body tightened, the finger touching her lip tensed. Unmistakable signs. Arousal. He didn't want it. Couldn't half believe it.

He also couldn't deny it.

Before he could decide what, if anything, he was going to do about it, Jillian stepped back and turned away. The moment dissolved instantly, making him wonder if he'd imagined it. He hadn't. But he had to admit it made him feel strange, sort of like having an out-of-body experience.

He shifted his weight, the twinge of pain in his thigh reassuring. He belatedly wondered if anything of what he'd begun to feel during that off moment in time had been reflected in his face. He doubted it. Keeping his expression unreadable was second nature.

Of course, so was maintaining complete control over his mental and physical responses—regardless of the stimulus. Lacking constant challenges, he was apparently getting rusty. His gaze wandered back to her again, completely detached now that she'd moved away. Rusty and desperate, he amended, chalking the whole thing up to repressed hormones and the combined events of the last several hours.

After quietly putting batteries into another flashlight, Jillian looked up at him. One glance into those steady eyes and he felt a tremor rock his sturdily built walls.

Lying to others had been part and parcel of his career, he'd done it many times without a flicker of remorse. It had saved his butt too many times for him to question the practice. But never, ever, had he lied to himself. No matter how harsh, it was the one and only truth he could count on.

Until now.

Because damn if he didn't want to pull her into his arms and find out how those warm, velvety lips would feel under his.

Weak. He was weak. And soft. A year ago he'd have never allowed himself to respond to *anyone* like this, much less a mousy little Yank. Abruptly he grabbed the last lantern and a package of batteries and hopped back to the table. The jolting pain was much stronger now. He'd been unaware of just when the Novocain had worn off.

Good. Pain he could handle. Solid, direct, mind-clearing pain.

Angling himself beside the chairs, he lowered himself and propped his foot up, not caring in the least what she thought about his actions as long as she stayed on the other side of the room for the next five minutes while he sorted things out.

"I'm guilty of the same thing, you know."

After the prolonged silence, her quiet statement grabbed his full attention. It probably shouldn't have. Careful to stay focused on his leg, he asked, "What's that?"

"Expecting others to act only in their own best interest. I may not like your methods, but I don't deny that you have principles. Although if you'd asked me an hour ago, I'd have refused to admit it."

A smile entered her voice, prompting him to look over at her. Even in the shadows cast by the lantern, he saw the soft curve of her lips. He found his own lips twitching in response and wasn't quite sure whether or not to stifle the rare notion.

Her smile faded before he could decide, his desire to smile evaporated along with it.

"I'm sorry our commitments got all tangled up," she said with convincing sincerity. "I know you didn't plan on getting caught out here." *With me.*

Reese wasn't sure if he heard those last two

words with his ears or with his mind. But either way, they'd come through loud and clear.

She tucked a flashlight under her arm and lifted a lantern in each hand. "I'm going to store some of these in the other rooms as a precaution. If you're hungry, I'll put together something to eat in a few minutes." She left the room before he could comment.

Which was just as well. Because in that exact instant, he realized that the adrenaline rush he'd felt, the challenge he'd perceived, had very little to do with the storm that was barreling down on them. And everything to do with the woman he was trapped in it with.

He doubted she'd have been happy to hear the string of words that revelation brought to his lips.

FOUR

Jillian glanced up the stairs, debating on whether it was worthwhile stowing a lantern on the upper level of the house. Another loud crack resounded outside, turning her head instinctively toward the front window. Damn, but it was frustrating not being able to see what was happening out there.

Compromising, she set the last lantern on the bottom step where it could be easily grabbed from either direction. Crossing her arms, she rubbed her hands over them, more in reaction to the turmoil surrounding the house than because she felt any chill. She hadn't thought the howling and moaning could possibly get any louder. The house seemed to vibrate from the noise alone. Maybe it was just as well she couldn't see outside. She'd done all she could to protect herself and the old house left to her by a father she'd barely known.

Jillian's mind flashed back over all the other

houses she'd lived in during her childhood. Each one bigger and more cavernous than the last as her mother remarried farther and farther up the income ladder. It was funny, but she couldn't seem to distinguish one from the other in her mind now. It was all just a bland, monochromatic blur of spacious, perfectly decorated rooms; full of style and taste, but empty of heart or soul.

She glanced around her, a smile coming to her lips. But this house . . . this old weather-beaten house had been her first, the one she'd been born in. Barely remembered, except for the ever-present feeling that it had been the only one that had ever felt like a home.

Jillian whispered a fervent prayer, asking the old house which had survived for almost thirty years, to hold out for another twenty-four hours.

Shutting out the old ghosts, she turned her mind to organizing a mental priority list of all the things she'd have to check on once the storm passed over. She shut out the possibility that she wouldn't be around to carry out the tasks. Nothing productive came out of negative thinking. She'd made that her motto the day she'd returned from Alaska four years ago; she'd be damned if she'd give it up now.

Her thoughts strayed back to the big Aussie in her kitchen. She'd meant every word she'd said to him. She hadn't wasted a second deciding whether she'd leave or not. But she'd certainly never meant for someone else to get trapped by a decision she'd made, no matter how unexpected the intrusion.

Dinner. They should eat now, just in case . . . She turned quickly on her heel and headed back down the short hallway connecting the small front parlor to the large country-style kitchen. She loved that room. Aside from her office in the converted garage/clinic, it was where she spent the most time. Yet she paused in the doorway.

Reese's back was to her, his shaggy blond head bent as he apparently examined her handiwork on his thigh. Her fingers twitched as she remembered the feel of his skin. There had been no give whatsoever, as if it were wrapped around marble. The stitches seemed even enough; she doubted the scar would be too noticeable when fully healed.

Allowing her gaze to drift over his broad shoulders, past his narrow waist, and down the length of the well-muscled leg propped on her kitchen chair, she couldn't help but wonder if he had other scars on his body. She knew—sensed—on some level she couldn't identify, that he did.

A shiver raced lightly over her skin. The sensation not chilling or unpleasant. She didn't know much about him. But what little she did know seemed to indicate a life led just outside the rules. She couldn't imagine him holding down some quiet, staid job, punching a time clock every day at five. Maybe it was the dramatic way they'd met.

No. This man had renegade written all over him. If the idea weren't so completely laughable, she might have even allowed herself a minute or two—or even ten—to imagine what it would be like to have a fling with an outlaw like Reese Braedon. To fantasize that the darkening of his blue eyes when he'd stared at her earlier had been the result of passion, not consternation.

She allowed herself a small smile. She wouldn't catch the attention of a man like Reese Braedon if she stripped down naked, waltzed into the kitchen and offered herself up to him like a turkey on Thanksgiving.

"I don't mind you standing there staring at me, but I figure we should eat before Ivan comes banging on the door."

Jillian hadn't thought a person's entire body could blush simultaneously. She'd guessed wrong. Total humiliation rooted her to the spot. Not even when she'd overheard Richard Laxalt regaling the rest of the Valdez project crew with the story of her infamous engagement—which she'd confessed to him in private because she thought he cared, truly cared, for her. Even then she hadn't felt this exposed.

"Never mind." He grunted as he started to lever himself up to a stand, the motion more than the noise grabbing her attention.

She hurried into the room. "Don't get up." Halfway toward him, hand outstretched to hold him down if necessary, she abruptly changed direction, heading instead to the pantry to the right of the hallway door. No way would she be able to touch him now. No matter how innocent the gesture.

Regardless of what happened in the next few hours, she was determined to stay as far away from Reese Braedon as possible. Those fantasy images had been all too vivid for her peace of mind. And for the last four years, she'd placed peace of mind above all other considerations.

Being stranded in a hurricane with a hunk—even a big, blue-eyed Australian hunk that could give Mel Gibson lessons on chemistry—was no reason to abandon that painfully learned creed. In fact, it was the best reinforcement for her current choice of lifestyle. If and when she decided to test the waters again, the very last person she'd try to wade out to would be an Aussie with an attitude.

Sighing in relief when he settled back in the chair, she stepped into the small shelved closet that held all of her canned goods and cooking supplies and set the flashlight on one end so she could see. She'd already decided to use up some of the lunch meat in the refrigerator, figuring she should save the canned food just in case things got desperate. She had stored three cardboard cartons full of emergency rations in the large storage closet in the hallway along with the medical supplies she'd carted in from the clinic, but it never hurt to be cautious.

She grabbed the bag of tortilla chips she'd opened the day before and a bag of sesame seed rolls and turned to leave, then remembered she had a can of prefab nacho dip stashed somewhere in here. She spared a half a second wondering what Reese would make of her less than nutritious eating habits before deciding she didn't care. Putting down the chips and bread, she began rooting through the shelves, eventually stepping up on an unopened can of shortening to grope around on the top shelf.

"Aha!" Just as her hand closed around the small round container, the can beneath her feet shifted. In the next instant, she lost her balance and fell in a painful heap on the floor of the pantry.

"What the hell are you doing in there?"

She'd managed to bang both elbows, one ankle-bone, and her fanny smarted like the dickens. "I'm fine, thanks," she called back, not bothering to hide the sarcasm. Wonderful, she thought, make him think you're a klutz as well as an idiot.

Discovering she still cared what he thought of her did little to improve her mood. "Don't bother getting up," she muttered as she gingerly rolled out of her awkward position.

"Too late."

She froze at the sound of his raspy voice, which was far too close to still be coming from the table. She stifled a groan and pieced together her control. She'd already made a complete fool of herself, but she'd be damned if she'd give him an encore.

"You shouldn't have gotten up." She tucked her feet under her and knelt, wincing despite her efforts not to when her knee pressed against the hard tile floor.

"So I heard."

Before she could comment, strong fingers clamped around her upper arm and helped her to a stand. As soon as she was steady on her feet, he let her go.

His hand had been hot against her skin. She ignored the lingering traces of warmth. Not wanting to risk looking him in the eye just yet, she gathered the bread and chips, then ducked back down to grab the can of dip she'd dropped when she'd fallen.

"I hope you're not into health food," she said as she straightened back up. Anything else she'd been about to say went unspoken as her gaze connected with his.

"If I can stomach Vegemite, I can handle anything."

His tone wasn't light or amused, yet he'd put her at ease. Or at least as much at ease as she could be staring into those eyes of his. Clear blue crystals, they captured her complete attention, despite her inner voice urging her not to be a fool twice.

"You okay?" The small pantry muted the storm noise, allowing the soft rasp of his voice to carry easily over the short distance between them.

"No. I mean, I'm fine. A few bruises." She wished he'd back out of the doorway. This was exactly what she'd wanted to avoid. She made a desperate stab at humor. "What is it you guys down under say? No worries."

He lifted his hand and reached forward, causing her to instinctively shift away, banging her sore elbow against the shelf beside her. "Ouch."

He reached past her and grabbed the flashlight. "Jillian?"

Not for all the money in the world would she look at him now. She rubbed her elbow, keeping her gaze on the floor.

A callused fingertip prodded her chin upward until she was looking at him again. She swore to herself that she'd rather run out into the heart of the storm than let him see embarrassment on her face, and used every scrap of control to paste a blank expression on it instead.

"Would you mind moving out of the way?" She was proud of the calm sound of her voice. So what if it wobbled a bit? "You should rest that leg, and I've got a meal to prepare. Such as it is."

Her attempt at lightening the sudden tension had failed miserably if his expression was anything to judge by. But then she hadn't had much luck reading him up till now, so who knew?

"Don't try so hard, mite."

With his accent she couldn't tell if he'd said "mate" or "mite." It didn't matter, either way it wasn't exactly flattering. No surprise there. The tension ebbed from her all at once as she realized how ridiculous this whole thing was. Her reaction to him, worrying about what he thought, when all she should be concerned with was surviving the storm so she could help Cleo.

"Yeah well, trying too hard is what I do best." She bent her knees, intending to duck under his arm.

He stopped that by bracing his arm lower on the doorframe. "Self-pity doesn't become you."

"As far as I can tell, nothing much becomes me, so tough darts. Please move."

"Are you afraid of the dark?"

"What?" His question caught her so off guard, she stopped trying to move his arm and looked up at him. "No," she answered, without knowing why.

"Good."

She heard the click of the flashlight, then the small pantry went dark. What little light reached them from the kitchen was almost completely blocked out by his large body filling the doorway.

"Come here."

She stood completely still, her brain racing so fast to make something out of the sudden change of events that she couldn't think at all. "Where?"

He sighed deeply. The next thing she knew she was pulled against his chest, her nose buried in the middle of the damp T-shirt stretched across the rock-hard wall of muscle.

Startled, she stood stock-still. He leaned against the door and pulled her closer against him with a brawny arm around her waist. His other hand dropped to her hair, thick fingers weaving through it until they brushed against her nape. He expertly tucked her cheek into the crook under his arm.

"Put your arms around me," he whispered.

Assailed with so many sensations she didn't know where to start cataloging their effect on her, she automatically lifted her arms in compliance, looping them loosely around his lean waist.

"Tighter."

She squeezed gently. And felt a distinct bulge under the back of his vest. His gun.

It hadn't occurred to her to wonder why he carried one.

Until now.

Like a life preserver in a storm-tossed sea, she grabbed ahold of that thought and hung on for dear life. "Reese?"

"Hmmm?" His voice was a low rumble. It sounded so good, she almost forgot what she'd been about to ask.

"Since when do evacuation team members carry guns?"

He stiffened, then dropped his arms and shifted away from her. She froze for a moment, her mind still trying to get used to the feel of him in her arms, unable to assimilate why she was suddenly standing alone. Then she stepped back into the pantry, instinctively seeking more space as she sorted through what had just happened between them.

One thing became clear right away. She was lucky she'd come to her senses before he had the chance to make a fool of her again. Or before she beat him to it. Funny how that revelation did next to nothing to make her feel better.

Not only had he become weak, Reese decided as he hobbled over to the counter, he'd become soft as well. And stupid.

What in the hell had he been thinking of back there?

Certainly not his job. Certainly not gaining control of the situation.

No. For one ludicrous moment, he'd wanted to find out just what it was about her that got to him. His eyes certainly weren't telegraphing the information. So in a moment of weakness, he'd shut off the light and pulled her against him, hoping his other senses would alert him to the problem area.

He'd had the ridiculous notion that once he'd figured out what it was about her that made his mind go blank and his pants grow tight, the problem would end. Knowledge was power. Power enabled control.

He felt rather than heard Jillian behind him. Leaning heavily against the counter, he shifted slightly so he could see her. She was still standing in the pantry doorway. Her small shoulders were squared, her chin lifted, her expression making it clear she was waiting for a response.

And the urge to pull her back into his arms, to feel her soften against him, to know he could throw her as off balance as she did him, was so strong, it took him a moment to remember what her question had been.

Oh yeah. The gun. He shrugged when he'd rather have hit something. "It's been with me a long time. Can't seem to leave home without it."

As tension breakers went, his apparently left much to be desired. Too damn bad. It was the best he could manage.

If she found it so easy to maintain her control, he was more than willing to let her call the shots for a while.

Remaining silent, he watched Jillian clutch the rolls, chips, and the can of dip to her chest like protective armor, and walk over to the opposite end of the counter. She carefully laid everything out, got a knife from the drawer in front of her, then moved silently to the fridge, reaching into its darkened depths and retrieving several bundles wrapped in white deli paper.

She'd made two sandwiches and was starting on the third when she finally broke the tense silence. "So, Mr. Braedon, just what is it you do?" She turned to look at him. "When you're not battling gators and rescuing reluctant damsels in distress?"

There was that pluck again.

Funny, it didn't bother him so much this time. So what if her tension breakers were better than his? He let his hands relax, unaware until that moment that he'd had them tightly clenched.

"Private security. My partner and I own a business down in the Keys."

Her eyes widened. "They evacuated already down there, didn't they?"

"Yep."

She went back to making sandwiches. "I guess you must think I'm really ungrateful. I'm sure you must have better things to worry about right now than running around evacuating other people."

Before Reese could comment, she looked at him.

"Just what brought you all the way up the Gulf Coast? Are you a volunteer with some organized national rescue effort?" She waved a mustard-covered knife in front of her. "I mean, did you have to come up here? You and your family must be worried about your property and all." She laid the knife down, real concern on her face. "And now they have to worry about you too. I'm really sorry, Reese. I never intended to let my decision to stay affect others."

Reese wished she would shut up. "No worries." His voice wasn't as casual as he'd have liked. "There is no family. Just Cole, my partner. And he knows I understood the risks when I took the job."

She took several steps toward him. When she laid her small hand over his, he realized he'd just lied again.

"Well, I still feel responsible. When this is over, if I can do anything to help . . ." Her words drifted away when he flipped his hand over and tucked his fingers between hers.

"Let's get through the next couple of hours first." He gave her fingers a light squeeze, then drew his hand away. "You got paper plates?" He hoped like hell they were on the other side of the room.

"Yes. In the pantry, second shelf on the right." He hopped once, and she put out her hand. "What am I doing? You sit. I'll get the plates."

He shrugged off her hand and hopped across the room. "Got a spare broom handle?" He braced one hand on the doorframe, but didn't look back.

"Behind the door on the rack."

The instructions were delivered in short, clipped words. He'd insulted her. Too damn bad. He yanked down a sponge mop and flipped it over. A little short but it would do. He lifted the flashlight from the shelf. She'd apparently forgotten it after . . .

His body tightened. She'd barely known what to do during those all-too-brief moments they'd held each other. It hadn't even been much of a hug. There was next to nothing to hold. Yet she'd fitted against him perfectly.

And damn if it hadn't felt good. Like something he'd like to try again.

He flicked the switch on, erasing the shadows from the small room. And his brain.

❖——————❖

Reese swallowed the last bite of his second sandwich, then drained the last of his soda. He tried not to shudder as the sweet lemon-lime drink slid down his throat.

"Sorry about the beer being warm. I thought it was better to use the room in the fridge for water."

"And soda."

She smiled. It was sort of shy and sweet. He balled up his napkin.

"I ranked space in order of priority. Soda ranks just under water and perishables."

He fought the urge to let the corners of his mouth twitch upward. "I'd put tinnies in the same place myself, so I guess I understand. I've gotten used to drinking them cold."

"Tinnies?"

"Beer in Australian. Comes in tin cans. Tinnies."

"Of course," she said dryly. "Silly me."

He lost the battle, but stopped his curving lips shy of a true smile. He figured he could relent a little without giving up any real measure of control.

"How long have you been in the States?"

It was a realistic question. To be expected, even. Reese just had to get used to talking to someone who asked questions like she really wanted to know the answers. For him, conversation with a woman was usually just meaningless chitchat, soon forgotten once he'd begun the sort of communication he really desired. The sort that consisted mostly of sighs and moans.

He found himself staring at her mouth, wondering what she'd sound like during sex. Did she make noise? His gaze drifted down over the barely raised front of her shirt. Did she even have sex?

What the hell did *he* care? He looked down at the table.

"Never mind. I guess it's none of my—"

"I left Australia when I was seventeen." Now why hadn't he just let her let him off the hook? Probably to get his mind off of the strange track it had just wandered down. Jillian Bonner in the sack would probably be as exciting as fondling a store mannequin.

So why did that feel like the biggest whopper he'd told himself yet?

Jillian stood abruptly and gathered the remains of their meal. "Would you like another?" She nodded at the empty can she held in one hand. "Maybe some water?"

"Pass. Got a radio?"

She nodded again and turned away to dispose of the trash, then hurried into the office.

Only after she'd disappeared from sight did Reese discover that his jaw was clenched shut so tightly, his teeth hurt. He was really slipping. The way she'd leapt from the table made him wonder what she'd seen in his eyes. No way could she have read his thoughts. Nothing of what he felt was reflected there. Not ever. He doubted he could reverse that trait if he tried.

So what had sent her gladly running for the cover of her office?

Disgusted with all this exhausting internal debate, he shoved away from the table and stood. Too late, he remembered his thigh. Several creative expletives escaped his lips before he pressed them together. He'd just grabbed the mop from its leaning place against the chair next to his when she came back into the room.

"I already had it tuned to the local news station, but because of the wind, the reception with the batteries is pretty erratic." She'd been fiddling with the knobs and only now looked at him. "What are you doing standing up?"

"I was just asking myself the same thing." He successfully hid the strain in his voice, but not the frustration.

"Why don't we go into the front room? There's a couch there, you can elevate your leg."

Just then the constant noise of the storm exploded overhead with a loud boom, followed by a screeching sound that set his teeth on edge.

"Holy—What was that?" Jillian was halfway to the back door before she remembered the steel bars and covered window. She spun around to face Reese. "What should we do now?"

Reese swore under his breath. The short burst of adrenaline the sound had sent spurting through him would probably see him up the stairs to check out the top floor for roof damage. But the price he'd pay after wasn't worth the risk of expending the energy on a probable nonemergency. "I don't think it was major. If anything had been severely damaged, the sound inside would have increased."

She was already at the hallway door. "I'm going to take a look."

"No."

Her steps faltered, and she looked back at him. "Excuse me, but this *is* still my house." The fierce set of his mouth combined with that empty, hard stare made her add somewhat defensively, "You said it was probably nothing serious."

"I said I thought the roof was still on, not that it wasn't serious." He grabbed the radio off the table. "You picked a safe spot to ride this thing out in?"

It took a second for her to switch mental tracks. "The hall storage closet."

"How big?"

"I don't know. It's a walk-in. I knocked out the wall between the old coat closet and had it enlarged. My office didn't have a closet, so—"

"Bigger than the pantry?"

Not until he cut her off had she realized she was rambling. *Get a grip*, she commanded herself. *You planned for this down to the last detail. It'll be okay.* Drawing in a breath, she squared her shoulders. "About twice the size. It's partly filled with medical supplies from my clinic office in the other building. There's also a few cartons of emergency rations and survival gear."

"Good." Tucking the sponge end of the mop under his arm, he moved surprisingly swiftly to her side. "Does the couch have cushions that can be removed?"

"Well, yes, but—"

"Good, I'll get them."

He started to squeeze past her, then stopped partway through the door. He looked at her, and she stopped breathing.

"You got a bedroom on this floor?"

"Do I . . . what?" Her voice trailed off into an embarrassing squeak, prompting her to swallow. Hard. He was much too close, and too . . . everything . . . to mention bedrooms. She wasn't proud to discover, at a time when she should be fearing for her very life, that he could inspire erotic thoughts with the mere mention of a stupid room.

So what if her old four-poster bed was in that room? The one that wouldn't fit up the stairs so she'd had to sacrifice it to the guest room.

"A bedroom. Down here." His voice was tight with impatience. He pronounced "here" like it had two syllables.

"The door off the foyer, at the base of the stairs." He paused for a moment, just staring at her. Her lips felt suddenly parched and dry. So she licked them.

The most remarkable thing happened next. His eyes actually changed color. Or maybe it was the rapid expansion of his pupils. And why in the hell was she noticing such a thing now? "I'll . . . uh, I'll get the cushions."

A thick forearm halted her attempt at a hasty retreat.

"I'll get the cushions. You strip the bed down to the mattress. I'll be in to help you move it." He dropped his arm, but didn't move out of her way, or stop staring at her.

What was stopping her from just shoving past him she didn't know or care to examine too closely. Possibly the knowledge that some part of her anatomy would have to come into contact with some part of his. And he had *some* parts.

"Single or double?"

"What?"

He jerked his head down the hallway.

"Oh, the bed. Queen."

"Good." Without another word, he dropped his arm and shifted back so she could precede him down the hall. It took most of her will not to break into a run. She swore she could feel him behind her just as surely as if he were touching her. "Ridiculous," she whispered under her breath, wondering wildly if there were any published reports about hurricanes and their effect on a person's libido.

FIVE

Reese watched her narrow hips and slight fanny swing down the hallway in front of him. Realizing he'd slowed down just so he could watch her go the entire length of the hall, he averted his gaze—and his thoughts—to set about making final preparations.

Once he had tossed the cushions into the storage closet, he went back down the hall to the front bedroom. Using the tip of the mop handle, he tapped the door open. Then stopped dead on the threshold.

Rationally, the sight of that same slight fanny stuck up in the air as she knelt on all fours while yanking at the far corner of the light blue linen shouldn't have affected him in the least. God, he should have had the beer warm. Five or six of them, at least. It was obvious he was losing his edge anyway. What possible harm could alcohol do to his system if one glance at her scrawny little butt had him wondering just how soft that mattress was?

"Come on, you tight little . . ."

The rest of her entreaty degenerated into swearing mixed with heated grunting as she pulled on the recalcitrant sheet. Damn, but she made him want to smile.

"Where'd you learn to swear like that, anyway?" he asked as he hopped into the room and grabbed the opposite corner.

"Alaska." She grunted and gave a mighty tug at the same moment Reese freed the other corner, sending her sprawling back into the center of the bed with the linens tangled between her legs.

It was all Reese could do not to crawl right in on top of her.

Well, hell, he thought, irritated with his body's insistent response to her, maybe he should just do it. Do it and get past it. He was probably going to die in the storm anyway. Maybe that was the problem. His body sensed the end was near and was simply demanding one last go round.

Jillian glanced up and caught his look, then hastily wadded up the sheet and tossed it to the floor. The speed with which she scrambled off the bed had him wondering if he'd spoken his thoughts out loud.

It was just as well she put an end to his wild notion before he gave it any serious consideration. He stifled a sigh as he bent at the waist to heave the mattress to one side. If he was going to come and go in one day, he'd like to leave with a big satisfied grin on his face.

He wasn't sure Jillian had the proper equipment —or experience—to give him that eternal smile.

He was distracted from his thoughts when she bent low over the mattress directly across from him to help shove. The position gave him a clear view straight down the front of her shirt.

Well, what do you know, he noted, taking in the view without a flicker of remorse, she did have boobs after all.

"You gonna stand there all day staring down the front of my shirt or are we going to move this mattress?"

Reese looked up at her, expecting the harsh expression her voice indicated he'd find. It was there. But mixed in with the flippant I-could-give-a-damn look was a thread of pained vulnerability that shook him up more than he cared to admit. Didn't she know survivors never revealed their weaknesses? Especially to a man like him?

His gaze dropped from her tempest-filled eyes, past her pressed-together lips, then with a will of its own, on down to the peep show below.

But it was when he noticed the white-knuckled grip she had on the mattress pad that he felt his face heat. He'd been ogling her like a man sizing up the interior of a new car, debating on whether to take it for a test drive.

Which was perfectly in character for him. So

why was he blushing for the first time in his thirty-three years?

He abruptly turned his attention back to the task at hand. He'd obviously overtaxed his thigh injury. The sweat beginning to bead on his brow, his heart's slight acceleration. All signs he needed to rest.

He swore under his breath as he took a good hold on the mattress. Not only had she managed to irritate him more than any female he'd ever met, she was also turning him into a compulsive liar. And a damn lousy one at that.

With a grunt and a vicious tug, he pulled the thick pad half off the bed, barely hopping back in time to keep from falling.

"What happened to a three count?" Jillian grumbled as she crawled back off the bed he'd just yanked her half across.

"Stop griping and help me get this thing upright."

She slanted him a tight look, but thankfully did as he said without comment.

Once they'd maneuvered the mattress out into the front room, Reese motioned her to change ends. "You pull, I'll push."

"How about I pull, and you and your attitude go to hell."

She'd muttered the words, but he heard her nonetheless. All things considered, he should have let it pass. After all, her curvy little butt wasn't the only one on the line, and time was short. Still, he leaned his end of the mattress against the wall and hobbled around to face her.

"You ought to be on your knees thanking God or whatever you believe in that I'm stuck here with you."

She actually had the nerve to roll her eyes at him. If she hadn't been using all her strength to keep her end of the mattress from crashing to the floor, he wasn't too sure she wouldn't have decked him. Or kneed him.

For some reason the sight of her struggling with the ungainly hunk of bedding made him even angrier. "What the hell did you think you were going to do all alone out here? Huh? What on earth possessed you to try and ride this thing out?"

"Yell at me later, okay? This thing is about a quarter century old, long before anyone invented lightweight coils."

He wanted to hit something. No, he wanted to strangle something. Someone. He growled at her, then hobbled back to his end without bothering to see if what he'd said had any effect on her. He knew better.

"Why are we doing this anyway?"

He let his head drop to rest on the thick width braced between his hands. "We're going to bend this thing into the storage room so that it covers our heads. That way, when your roof caves in, we'll have a passing fair chance of not getting our skulls bashed in." He'd made the entire statement through clenched teeth. He raised his head and angled it to one side so he could see her. "Now can we get on with it? If I wanted to die on a mattress, it sure as hell wouldn't be this way."

Jillian ducked back behind the safety of her end of the mattress. Her face flamed even as she damned herself for letting him get to her. Her lips twisted in a rueful grin. Yeah, she imagined she was the very last type of woman a man like Reese would fantasize about spending his last minutes on earth with. To her eternal shame she couldn't say the same thing about him.

She vented her frustration on the task at hand. In less than a minute they had the mattress in front of the door. She stepped into the closet and quickly arranged the pillows in a framework around the edges of the room.

"No, pile them in the middle. We've got to move the boxes around the edges as support."

Jillian understood his plan. She quickly began rearranging boxes in stacks at each corner of the room, not bothering to tell Reese to sit down. She was only half surprised that his thigh wound and the necessary mop-handle crutch were barely noticeable impediments as he efficiently arranged twice as many boxes as she had in half the time.

Of course, if she'd stop gawking at him . . . his shoulder muscles and biceps flexing as he shoved boxes around, the way his jeans cupped his nice, tight . . . Sighing in disgust, she heaved the last box into place, then stood and wiped her damp palms on her jeans.

"Okay, what next?"

"Round up as much stuff from the kitchen as we can."

They were back in the storage closet in under ten minutes. Jillian stowed the lanterns and flashlights where she could reach them. Reese shoved the cooler they'd filled with the contents of the fridge off to one side, then ducked back into the hall and started shoving bottled water through the door. She stacked them neatly along another wall.

Once everything had been moved in, she turned in a slow circle and surveyed the space. The boxes were stacked about four feet high at the corners, three feet in between, with a row that would form a tower in the middle once the mattress was inside.

Even with the water, cooler, and lanterns, they had plenty of space, she noted with satisfaction.

A loud grunt had her spinning around.

"A little help here?"

She instantly moved to the door and grabbed one side of the mattress Reese was shoving into the room. She really liked the way he said the word "here" she mused as she struggled to make the thick pile of foam bend the way she wanted it to. Something about a man with an accent—

"Not that way!"

—Made her want to commit murder. "Which way would his highness like the slave girl to move it?" she asked with false obeisance.

"Sweetheart, if you were my slave, the last thing you'd need to ask me is how to move it."

Jillian clamped her mouth shut. At least he spared her a leering grin. Probably too busy trying not to laugh. She hoped he'd bust a gut. Reese grunted as he squeezed into the room. The mattress was bent almost in half, with the curve butting against the top of the doorframe.

"I'm going to wedge my body back into the fold and drag it forward," he instructed, still studying the doorway. "You face me and pull the edges. As it comes into the room, spread the sides out. Then we can prop one side up at a time."

"Sounds like a plan," she responded. Reese apparently didn't need her approval as he was already cramming his broad shoulders into the tight fold of foam.

Jillian was a foot away when it occurred to her that, initially at least, in order to grab the edges and pull, she'd have to all but thrust her chest into Reese's face.

Meager problem though it might seem, the prospect didn't thrill her. Telling herself he'd probably never even notice, she moved toward him, waiting until he ducked his head before she grabbed hold as best she could.

"Okay, pull."

Determined to get this over with as quickly as possible, Jillian put her back into it and yanked hard. Unfortunately she caught Reese off balance and along with a foot of mattress, she got Reese right where she didn't want him. Between her breasts.

"Whatever happened to a three count?"

It took a second for his muffled words to register. She was too busy praying her nipples wouldn't betray her reaction to having Reese's lips pressed in their near vicinity.

"Jillian?"

She wasn't certain, but she thought she might have groaned. When he spoke, the words vibrated against her skin. His lips were entirely too close to her . . .

"Mmmm?"

"If it were up to me," he said calmly into her shirt, "I'd spend the next several hours right here. But if we're going to survive the storm, you're gonna have to move back."

"Huh?" Then his words penetrated her suddenly fogged brain. What in the world had she been doing?

Standing there reveling in the feel of Reese Braedon's lips on her chest, was what she'd been doing.

Well jeez, a tiny voice inside her head retorted, it was probably the only chance she'd get.

"Jillian!"

Dear Lord, she was still doing it! Mortified, wishing Ivan would descend and pluck her off the face of the earth, Jillian leapt backward. Unfortunately, she also let go of the mattress.

"Holy mother of—" Reese's curse was cut short

when he catapulted into the room, the mattress on his back adding unwanted velocity.

"Reese! Look out! Slow—oof!"

In the next instant Jillian no longer had to worry about the secret thrill of having Reese's face pressed between her breasts. It was nothing compared to the feel of the full length of his hard muscled body on top of hers. Shoulder to belly to toe contact.

He lifted up on one elbow. She clenched her eyes shut to keep from seeing his expression, certain it was only going to make the awkward moment worse.

"You okay?"

He hadn't shouted at her. He wasn't swearing. In fact, he sounded downright . . . sincere. She cracked open one eye.

"Fine," she managed to whisper. "Pillows broke my fall." She swallowed. "You?"

"Well, this is the first time I've ever pinned a woman under a mattress."

He wasn't smiling at her. But his tone was gentle. The only time she'd heard that tone from him had been those few dark moments in the pantry.

"Why did you hug me?" The question just popped out.

Reese hadn't moved a muscle since he'd landed on top of her. "This isn't hugging. This is called breaking a fall."

"No, I mean in the pantry. Earlier." Using all of her nerve, she turned her head so their noses almost touched, her gaze locked dead on his. "Why did you turn the light off?"

Whatever light had penetrated his normally lifeless blue eyes blinked out. Jillian felt his body tighten, until he felt like stone on top of her.

"Never mind," she said quickly, damning herself for giving in even that small fraction. "Can you move?" she asked brusquely. "Is your leg hurt?"

His answer came after a lengthy pause. "I'll live. I'm going to push up on my hands and raise the mattress. Slide out and scoot over to the boxes we saved for the middle support and shove one over toward me."

Without waiting for her to answer, he lifted his weight from her. She sighed with relief and scrambled away as quickly as she could, taking care not to bang against his bad leg. In a matter of minutes they had the mattress propped up on the corner stacks, the center stack raising the middle high enough for them to sit without having to hunker down.

Jillian sat cross-legged on one side of the small space, and Reese stretched out his legs toward her from the other. The tear in his jeans caught her eye, thankfully giving her something to do.

"I'd better have a look at your thigh."

"Fair's fair."

She glanced at his face. There was that quiet tone again. It was hard to tell with him, but she knew he was teasing her. The good kind though, the kind that made her belly feel warm.

She smiled at him, deciding she'd better learn how to handle his quixotic brand of charm fast since she was stuck in this crawl space with him for God only knew how long.

"You think looking down my shirt was a fair trade?"

His eyebrows lifted slightly. She'd surprised him with that one. Good.

Not willing to push her luck, she scooted over to his side and bent her head to examine his wound.

"Could you move the flashlight over this way a few inches?" She motioned with one hand, but didn't look up. He didn't reply, but the light shifted. "Stop. Good." She moved the torn fabric away and peeled back part of the bandage. "It's red and there's been a bit of bleeding, but none of the stitches popped."

"You do right good work."

She looked up at him then. "Thank you." He looked at her in a way that made the warm feeling in her stomach dip a bit lower, and burn a bit brighter. She cleared her throat. "Let me get you something a bit stronger for the pain." She started to scoot away, but his hand on her arm stopped her.

"I'm okay. Just sit still. Relax."

She laughed without thinking whether or not she should. "Easy for you to say."

"I know you're worried," he responded, mis-reading her meaning. "You'd be a fool not to be. But don't add me to your list, all right?"

She looked down at his hand on her arm. His

fingers were rough, scarred, his skin darker than hers. She watched them rub gently along her forearm. In the next instant his hand dropped away. She looked up at him, and it hit her that her attraction to him was more than simply physical. Sometimes, like now, she'd look in his eyes and find something . . . familiar.

"You don't like people caring about you, do you? Why, Reese? Do you think that makes you weak?"

She'd asked him seriously, but as soon as the words were out she wondered if she should have given voice to her thoughts. He waited several moments, holding her gaze the entire time, until she was certain he wasn't going to answer. But he did.

"Not weak. Just less self-sufficient."

"And being completely in control is important to you?"

"It used to be the difference between breathing and dying."

"Used to be?"

He didn't move so much as a hair, but she sensed the sudden restlessness her question sparked.

"You're one to talk," he said finally. "Everything you've done today tells me you feel the same way. Your walls are pretty sturdy. What's your reason?"

Now it was her turn to feel restless. "Not the same as yours, I imagine."

Reese nodded, knowing Jillian's response was

an unspoken request not to push the subject any further. He gladly complied, not at all comfortable with this conversation—or the woman he was having it with. And yet, he found himself unwilling to let the matter drop entirely.

"Why didn't you evacuate?"

"For Cleo."

"Cleo. The alligator?"

"Yup."

"You mind explaining why you'd risk your life for a reptile?"

Reese winced inwardly when her expression became shuttered again. Too late, he recalled her words in the kitchen earlier. Now she thought he was just another coldhearted bastard who didn't respect life in all its forms.

And, to a degree, she was right. He respected life, the right everyone had to live their own. But to do his job, to survive, he'd had to remain carefully detached from the rest of it. It was just that he'd never been bothered by that truth until just this moment.

"You tell me why you carry a gun and look at me like you can't decide if I can be trusted—with what I don't know—and I'll explain why it's so important to me to follow through with my commitment to Cleo. I imagine we'll be equally unsuccessful."

Obviously considering the matter closed, Jillian turned toward her side of the small space.

"I hugged you in the pantry because I thought you needed one."

Jillian froze, holding as still as if he'd taken hold of her arm again, stunned by his admission. "You don't strike me as the type to give comfort."

He shrugged. But even more telling, he looked away from her.

She was crossing a mine field here, but she felt compelled to traverse the rest rather than retrace her steps. She turned completely and bent her knees, circling them with her arms and propping her chin on top. "You bark and roar like it's second nature, you order and command and expect immediate compliance. I imagine that all has to do with the reason you carry a gun. But you can also be nice."

His expression had grown quickly dark with her mini-analysis, but that last comment raised his eyebrows. "Me? Nice? What a horrible thing to say."

She smiled. "See, you can tease. It doesn't come easily to you."

Reese's expression darkened further. "Do you psychoanalyze all your patients, Doc?"

"Know what I think?"

"If I lie and say yes will you spare me?"

"I think you turned the light out in the pantry because you needed a hug too."

"I strike you as a shy type? A man who can't take what he wants in the light of day?"

"Darkness is as much a mental cloak as a visual

one. In the dark it's easier not to examine motives. It's easier to give in to instinct."

"Ah, who are we talking about now, Jillian?" His voice was a rough purr, and as dangerous as a mountain cat. "What instincts do you give in to only in the dark?"

The way Reese said her name, with the soft Aussie twang, made it wonderfully exotic instead of plain and ordinary. She didn't mind that he'd avoided commenting on her theory. She'd hardly expected a confession.

She pressed her lips against her folded hands, thinking about his question. She knew he was deflecting her, trying to put her on the defensive. It didn't take a genius to figure out she was uncomfortable with her sexuality. And Reese was far from stupid. But she answered him anyway.

"I try not to give in to instincts at all, dark or light."

"Then we are very different people."

"Why, because you let yourself be guided by instinct?"

"I'm alive today for that reason. But that's not what I meant."

"Then why do you think we are so different?"

"Because we both rely on instinct to save us. Only I don't lie to myself about it."

Before she could answer, he leaned forward and ran a rough-tipped finger down the length of her nose, letting it rest on her bottom lip.

"The question is, mite, what do you think you're saving yourself from?"

The shock of his unexpected caress, the pressure of his finger on her lip had her answering without thought to what she revealed. "Pain. Myself."

"Is it working?"

She lifted her head and pulled away from his touch. "Yes." *Until now.*

Jillian scooted back to her side of the small space, then rummaged in the cooler for a soda. As she wiped the condensation off the cold aluminum, she wondered if she'd be lucky enough to survive the storm, only to fall prey to her own foolish reaction to Reese.

"Slide the radio over here. Maybe we can find out what's going on outside."

A sigh of relief breathed out as she did as he asked. She'd rather listen to damage reports and the very real possibility that her home was going to be destroyed than sit in this small shadowed closet and dredge up painful memories best left buried and then trust them to the care of a man like Reese Braedon.

Static filled the stuffy room, and Jillian caught herself smiling as Reese swore very colorfully while he fiddled with the knobs.

"Is everyone in Australia as inventive as you when it comes to foul language?"

He spared her a brief glare, then returned to his

efforts. "I'd ask if that was an insult, but I've heard you swear, so I'll take it as professional curiosity."

This time she did laugh. And caught Reese's complete, immediate attention. "What?" she asked, surprised by the intensity of his reaction.

He bent his head again. After several long seconds in which he grumbled under his breath, he said, "Your laughter. Sounds nice."

That warm feeling stole into her belly again, and she didn't even bother trying to squelch it. Reese being sincere *and* nice at the same time was simply too irresistible.

"Thank you. Feels good too. You ought to try it sometime."

He didn't respond and as Jillian stared at the top of his blond head, she had the strangest notion that he might want to, but didn't know how. Or had forgotten how somewhere along the way.

She couldn't decide if that idea made her want to tease a smile from him. Or take him in her arms and hold him.

Just then a deep voice pierced the silence.

". . . heading up the Gulf Coast just off land, picking up speed over the open water. Ivan is expected to hit land just north of Marco and the Ten Thousand Islands region around nine o'clock this evening. The entire area from Ten Thousand Island area to the south of Venice has been evacuated, but no matter where Ivan hits, potential damage to property has been estimated to possibly reach well into the millions."

Just as suddenly as it had spurted to life, the newscast reverted to static. Jillian lifted her eyes from the radio to Reese.

"It'll be okay, Jillian. We'll make it."

In the next instant a tremendous crash reverberated through the house with enough force to rattle the stacks of boxes holding up the mattress.

Jillian instinctively ducked and threw her hands over her head. Reese reacted instinctively as well. Before the echoes had died out, he'd leaned forward and grabbed her by the shoulders. Pulling her half under him, he used his body as a shield in case the roof came down on them.

"Reese?" Her voice was as shaky as her nerves.

Resting on his good hip, he tucked her closer to his chest, his wounded leg between hers. He looked down at her, then reached up to smooth her bangs from her forehead.

"I think we're okay."

"Good." His hand felt strong and reassuring against her cheek. It wasn't until he ran his fingers over her lips that she realized he was trembling too.

"Reese?" She said it so softly, she wasn't sure he'd heard it.

"Hmmm?" His gaze was steady on her mouth.

"I think I could use another one of those hugs."

His finger paused, then withdrew. Jillian braced herself for him to withdraw the rest of his body from her as well.

Instead he reached behind her head and flicked off the light. The room pitched into total darkness.

In the next instant, he gathered her into his arms and pulled her firmly against his chest. Then, as if that wasn't close enough, he used his foot to tuck her legs tighter against him.

She felt his chin come to rest on the top of her head. Only then did it occur to her what he'd admitted by turning off the light.

"Thank you," she whispered against his chest.

His arms tightened briefly. "No problem."

And with his heart pounding strong and steady beneath her ear, she let her hands steal around his waist, and hugged him back.

SIX

Reese thought he knew every level of hell. He was wrong.

But unlike the other trials he'd endured over the past ten years, this form of torture was exquisite agony. Offering pleasure as its temptation, all the while knowing that the man desperate enough to reach for it would damn himself as a fool for eternity.

This lesson Reese understood. Painfully. Intimately.

And yet he laid there in the dark, the noise of the storm raging over his head like a thousand Valkyries screeching at him to run fast, run far, run forever . . . he laid there and continued to hold Jillian Bonner in his arms.

And when he felt her small hands sneak around his waist, he knew fool was the least of the names he'd call himself.

Reese shut out the voices inside his head, shut out the deafening sound of the storm outside, and concentrated on the feel of the woman in his arms.

Jillian couldn't have known how right she was about the cloak of darkness. Or maybe she did. He hadn't. Not until now. He'd acted on instinct both times he'd shut off the light—only now he understood the motivation wasn't as simple as defining his attraction to her. It went deeper than that, was riskier than that, powerful enough that he'd grasped for whatever was available as a defense. Darkness was the only shield he had, so he'd used it.

Her body was so small. He dwarfed her, he felt as if he could wrap himself completely around her. Protect her.

Damn it to bloody hell. So he wanted to protect. After all, it *was* his job. The one and only thing he was good at—both his saving grace and his eternal curse.

But the very last thing he wanted—ever, ever again—was to *need* to protect.

And yet he wanted.

Her breasts, so soft and small, pressed against his rib cage. Her slender legs fit perfectly between his larger, heavily muscled ones. Her small hands . . . He stifled a groan. Her wonderfully skilled hands were those of a healer. And damn if they didn't bring him a sense of solace he'd never expected to feel. Never expected because it wasn't deserved.

Still, he wanted. He wanted till he fair burned with it.

"Jillian?" His voice was hoarse with the effort to speak at a time when his body was screaming at him to act.

She shifted slightly against his chest, and he ground his teeth together. She started to draw her hands away, but no matter how deeply he understood that he should allow her to put some space— any space—between them, there was no way in hell he was going to let her. Not yet.

He pressed his elbows down, clamping her arms to his sides. She tensed, then stopped. He sighed, the sound filled with as much frustration as relief.

"What?" she whispered.

"Tell me why you risked your life for Cleo." Again, his voice was dark and rough, but it was all he could manage.

"Another order, Mr. Braedon?" Her tone was dry, but not angry, as if she somehow understood how vital it was for him to reestablish the space between them—even if it was only verbal.

"Curiosity, Ms. Bonner. You don't strike me as a person to put herself in unnecessary danger."

Reese felt her tense. He wondered if she realized that by being in his arms she'd placed herself directly in the path of another fierce, potentially dangerous storm. That of desire. Surprising, unexpected, but no less powerful than the one pounding down on them.

Reese called on what control he had to keep his

hold on her relaxed, to keep the heart beating under her cheek steady.

"Normally, I'd be the first to agree," she said, the wry quality more evident now.

Good on you, mite, he thought, satisfied that the survivor instinct was still alive and strong inside her.

"What made Cleo different?" *What made me different?* was what he really wanted to ask. He swallowed hard against the urge.

After a pause, her voice floated up to him in the darkness, clear and steady.

"She was brought to me several months ago. Her rear left leg had been almost completely severed in a steel trap designed to catch small mammals."

"Why you?"

"Why not me?"

"You said you weren't a vet. I guess I just figured you'd leave the bigger cases to the government wildlife folks. You have a staff here?"

"I have a few volunteers. Cleo was brought here because I was the closest person available. Around here it's catch as catch can. She wasn't an endangered species, and while there are several breeding programs currently underway, she wouldn't have rated special attention. It was either me or leave her to die. If they'd taken her even as far as Sanibel, she wouldn't have survived."

"So she was a goner when she got here, huh?"

"The guys in the pickup truck that brought her in thought so."

"But not you." It wasn't a question. He knew her well enough now to realize that nothing short of death—even her own apparently—would stop Jillian from doing whatever she thought she had to do.

"Actually, I thought it would be over before we got her from the truck to the clinic. I sedated her to keep her down and went to work on her leg. As you said, I'm no vet. But even I knew the leg had to go."

"Wait a minute . . ."

"Yes, Cleo was the one I was referring to when I was stitching you up."

"You mean the scaly bludger that attacked me only has three legs?"

Jillian laughed. "Don't feel bad, Reese. She still moves pretty darn fast. Usually it's in the other direction when humans are involved. Most alligators prefer smaller, easily captured meals and since they're cold-blooded, they are notorious for not expending any unnecessary energy."

"So why attack me?"

"The only time alligators—at least this species —get aggressive to the point of unprovoked attack is when their nests are involved. And Cleo is a very protective mother-to-be."

"I wasn't anywhere near the pond or the nest."

"I've thought about that. Females usually stay very close to their egg mounds during incubation, but I guess maybe the winds and impending storm confused her or agitated her. She must have been on the other side of the compound, and you just had the bad misfortune of coming between her and her nest."

"If you let her roam free, you should have signs up."

"I do. Or at least, I did. The winds must have blown them down. This is a pretty isolated area. I don't have that many guests other than those who are bringing in injured animals. If they know about me, they more than likely know about Cleo. Even so, I hooked up a buzzer and an intercom on the gate. I guess you didn't see it."

Her tone made it clear that she didn't think he'd taken the time to look before barging in, but Reese didn't comment. Mostly because she was right. But also because he wasn't ready to give her an excuse to leave the shelter of his arms. He knew she'd stayed this long only because he'd kept her talking.

"I still don't understand why you stayed. Do you have other animals still here?"

"No. I was very fortunate. Besides Cleo, I only had several waterfowl here when the storm warnings were announced. I have an arrangement with another rehabber near Ocala who takes on birds when I don't have enough space. Luckily she had room and took them on for me."

"You couldn't move Cleo?"

"Actually, I'd planned to release her back into

the wild. She seemed to have adapted to her new limitations well enough, and I checked with the U.S. parks people on the best place to put her. But before I could arrange it, she started building her nest. If everything goes well, we'll transport them all after they hatch."

Reese paused for a moment, trying to decide how best to ask the next question. "Don't do a lolly, but if she's not endangered, why not move her anyway? One less egg mound wouldn't hurt the population."

"Do a lolly?"

"Tantrum, fit."

It was Jillian's turn to pause. It went on just long enough for Reese to start to feel uncomfortable. He hadn't been self-conscious about his accent or Australian background in over sixteen years, since he'd first hit the back alleys of Miami as a rebellious teenager fresh from Oz. That he felt that way now spoke volumes on how much he'd let Jillian get to him. They were volumes he'd as soon leave unread.

"I'm not going to 'do a lolly,' " she replied, imitating him, the soft accent on her lips breaking gently into his thoughts. "It's a valid question."

Reese fought his initial reaction, which had been to smile. Then realizing she couldn't see it, allowed his mouth to relax a bit, his lips curved slightly. "For a Yank, you do a passing fair job of speaking Strine."

He didn't have to see her smile. He felt it. She

smiled with her whole body. His body had passed smiling eons ago, it was well into pleading. He ignored it. But not without paying a dear price.

"So why didn't you leave her here?" he asked quietly. "Not much you can do barricaded in the house."

Her arms tightened around his waist, and Reese used what was left of his control not to roll on top of her and the hell with the conversation. But he sensed her hold on him was prodded by the need for reassurance, not barely restrained passion.

Double bloody hell.

"Tell me."

At his roughly spoken request, she started to pull away. He held her tighter, the action automatic.

"Don't run."

"I can hardly do that in here, now can I?"

"You know what I mean."

She wedged her arms between them and pushed. "Yes, I do." She struggled again. "Dammit, Reese, you're asking me to—You're asking for more than a simple explanation."

He'd placed his lips next to her ear, so his whisper could be heard over the noise of the storm. "Am I?"

Jillian's response was to fight harder. Reese relaxed his hold, but just enough so that she could roll away from him, then he caught her around the waist with one arm and pulled her back against him.

"Reese, wh—?" She flailed around momentarily. "Let me—" She broke off when her backside encountered the hard line of his hips. "—go." The last word was nothing more than a whisper. He felt the vibration of it against his body.

Forcibly preventing himself from examining his motivations, he held on tight as he bent his head, placing his lips by her ear again.

"Darkness is a cloak. So is facing an empty room."

"Let me go." The words were raspy, but the only plea was for understanding.

"You want a shield. You've asked me for one twice. That's all my arms around you are. Protection. Respite. A shield. Now, shut your eyes and let the words out, Jillian." His mouth opened against the shell of her ear. "Tell me why a survivor like you would willingly do something so self-destructive."

He let his lips graze the tender skin of her neck, swallowing hard on the groan that rose from the depths of his chest and lodged in his throat. "Tell me."

Reese wasn't aware he'd been holding his breath along with the need to groan, until several excruciating moments passed and she relaxed against him. He sensed she was more resigned than willing, but he was past caring. With the remains of his control, he pulled his mouth away from the tantalizing scent of her nape and tucked her head back beneath his chin. *Where it belonged.*

"I . . . um." Jillian paused to clear her throat. Never in a million years did she expect to be having this conversation with a man like Reese, but to be doing it with her bottom pressed against his zipper went beyond all comprehension. She purposely let her gaze become lost in the dark room in front of her. "I guess it's part of what I said earlier, about people's motivations being self-serving. Animals aren't that way. Their motivation is simple, basic. It's to survive."

"And reproduce."

She drew in a ragged breath. "Yes, and that."

"So you're saying that the animals you treat are more loyal or appreciative? Ducks, snakes, alligators?"

"Not in the way you mean, maybe. Not like a pet. I guess I just like knowing that my efforts will give them the one thing they desire above all else— to live. No power games, no hidden agendas, no regrets."

Jillian's pulse pounded inside her ears as the silence between them grew. She purposely allowed the sounds of the storm to reenter her mind, trying not to think about what his next question was almost certainly going to be.

But the storm took a poor second in her thoughts to the feel of Reese's arms around her, the feel of his silent strength braced behind her. It was surprisingly reassuring. Not the protection he offered from the dangers of the raging hurricane, she knew he had an instinctive code to protect.

What captured her attention was the fact that the feel of his body wrapped around her provided far more than a cloak to hide in while revealing past hurts. It made her feel safe. Truly safe. Able for the first time, to sort out the events that had shaped her life, driven her down her chosen path. He enabled her to be vulnerable without fear that whatever she said would be twisted around and used against her.

The knowledge didn't require thought and decision. It was solely instinctive. Why? For the past four years she'd successfully, easily, shut off any emotion she deemed risky to her heart. To her soul. Giving that part of herself only to her patients, whose existence in her life was temporary by necessity. The result had provided her with a tremendous sense of relief. She'd never regretted her decision to isolate herself. In fact, she'd reveled in it. And she'd sworn she'd never do anything to disturb it. Ever.

Apparently until now.

So why Reese? Because he was very likely the last man, the last human being, she'd talk to before the storm swept them both away? Because he'd bullied his way into her life and didn't take no for an answer? Because she saw a soul mate when she looked into his battle-weary blue eyes?

Or was it because he made her feel female in a way that only someone so supremely male ever could have? In a way she'd never ever expected to feel?

Yes. Maybe. She didn't know.

Most telling, in that moment, was that she didn't care.

"Who abused your trust, Jillian?"

The question drifted into her mind on a raw whisper.

"Who abused your heart?"

After a long pause, she said, "I think it would be easier, not to mention faster, to name those who hadn't. I'm apparently a lousy judge of character. Although that doesn't excuse my mother. I didn't get the option of choosing her."

As if doors too long closed had suddenly sprung open, she'd spoken in a heated rush. Only when the relative silence of their small space descended once again did she realize what she'd said, what she'd revealed.

Reese relaxed, letting his hand drift to her arm. He drew his rough hand along the taut skin that stretched from her elbow, over her slight bicep muscle, to her shoulder. He paused for a split second, then repeated the excruciatingly exquisite gesture as he let his hand drift back down.

"You want to tell me about it?"

The question, though expected, sent her over some unforeseen edge. Everything shattered apart.

His voice, that accent, those arms. His hands, his body, his strength. The dark, the storm, the small room. His scent, his zipper, the unmistakable bulge behind it. Her pulse, her want, the need to turn in his arms and . . .

Oh my God. What in the hell was she doing?

Suddenly Jillian wanted out. Away from Reese, away from the way he made her feel, away from the things she wanted to say. Away from the things she wanted to do.

She wanted light. Air. Blessed quiet. Both outside and in her head.

As if he'd sensed her thoughts, Reese's arms tightened around her. "Okay, okay. None of my business."

Jillian worked hard to school her breath to an even pace, willing herself not to panic like her mind was screaming at her to do. "Your turn," she said at length, her voice hoarse.

Now he tensed. And suddenly she wanted to smile. To laugh out loud. What a hell of a pair they made.

"Nothing horrible," she assured him. "What made you decide to come to America?"

He remained tense. "Ask another question."

"Okay. None of *my* business. Can you tell me what you did before you opened your private security firm?"

Silence. Still stiff. She had the odd thought that now it felt like a tree was hugging her.

"If I guess will you tell me?"

His arms loosened a bit. His chest relaxed, and she felt his heart drop into a steady rhythm.

"You don't think I can, do you?"

"You're free to try."

"If I'm right, will you tell me?"

"I'll never lie to you."

Jillian tensed at the quiet declaration, then forced herself to relax in his arms. "You carried a gun then as you do now. I think it's like an extension of you. So the easy guess would be a cop. But that wasn't it."

"What makes you say that?"

His tone was one of reluctant interest. Jillian allowed herself a secret smile. It was so much nicer now that her turn was over. "You don't strike me as a man who'd settle for solving local problems." He tensed again, but it didn't daunt her. "I mean, even now, you're tackling this hurricane like someone who would vanquish it single-handedly if he could. I can't see you giving out speeding tickets or investigating the robbery of the local five-and-dime."

"For a lousy judge of character, you have a passing fair amount of intuition."

"So what made you quit, Reese?"

"Who said I quit? I changed jobs." She felt him shrug.

"Are you happier now?"

Another long pause. "I don't think happiness ever played a role in any decision I've made in over sixteen years."

His tone was flat and resigned. A tiny ache knotted her insides way down deep in a place she'd kept scrupulously closed to inspection. "I'm sorry, Reese."

"Odd, coming from you."

"What makes you say that?" she asked, honestly

surprised at his remark. "I'm happy. I love what I do."

"I like what I do too. We're both good at our jobs, and I imagine we both derive equal amounts of satisfaction from them. But job satisfaction isn't happiness, Jillian."

"Then what do you call it?"

"Surviving."

A shiver ripped through her. And that hollow space in the pit of her soul suddenly yawned open, the black emptiness echoing with the truth of his assessment. Surviving.

"Maybe," she said, so softly, she wasn't certain he could hear her. "But I'm pretty damn happy with that. It beats the alternative."

In the next instant she was facing Reese. He turned her over and pulled her up until her face was just breathing space away from his.

"Too right, mite. Too right." He lowered his mouth toward hers, then in the instant before they would have touched, he pulled back an inch and whispered, "So tell me, why is it that I'm suddenly not so satisfied with just surviving?"

Jillian wasn't given the chance to answer. A breath later she'd forgotten she wanted to.

His lips were warm and firm; the tip of his tongue, wet and hot. He didn't devour her, he didn't crush her lips with his as she'd half expected —as she wanted to do to him.

He tasted her, sampled her, moved his mouth over her lips slowly and so thoroughly, she memorized every texture and taste of his. He plundered her mouth, stealing her tongue and carrying it back into his own, where he savored it as if it were a much-sought-after treasure.

Never had she been so completely seduced by a simple kiss. Except there was nothing simple about Reese's kiss.

There was nothing simple about Reese.

His hands had been holding her arms, but as he slanted his mouth to take the kiss even deeper, he moved one hand around her waist, his big palm spanning the small of her back as he pulled her more tightly against him. His other hand slid slowly up her arm. She arched violently against him as the back of his thumb dragged against the side of her breast.

Reese groaned as his body responded in kind. "Madness," he whispered raggedly against her lips. "Stop me, Jillian. You won't find happiness here. Not with me."

"Neither will you," she rasped back, the teasing feel of his lips just beyond hers almost as seductive as actually tasting them. "But maybe we can have pleasure. Surely we each deserve some pleasure."

Reese pushed his hand into her cropped-off hair, the thick pads of fingers performing the most erotic massage on her scalp. He gripped her head gently and pulled it back, leaning over her so that when he spoke his hot breath whispered straight into her open mouth and down her throat.

"Yeah, but haven't you learned that the pain that always follows is never worth the thrill?"

The storm boomed into the sudden breach in their hushed conversation, rattling the house, shaking the very floor beneath them. Jillian realized how far gone she was when she merely reveled in the heightened sensations the undulating rhythm of the flooring provided.

"This time we may not be around long enough for the pain." Her voice was a hoarse rasp. "But I know I can have pleasure, Reese. Now. With you." She heard him suck in his breath, felt his rib cage rub against her belly. She swallowed a moan. "We're both survivors, Reese. We'll deal with the fallout after."

Reese's answer was to take her mouth again. And again. Where before there had been sweet, sinful seduction, there was now only hot, driven possession. His mouth ravaged hers as if the storm outside had entered the very room, had taken up residence in his body.

Jillian gripped his shoulders, twisting her hips in search of an elusive fix, something, anything to take the ache away. The thought had barely formed when she felt the hard shell of his denim-clad knee push between her legs.

Oh yes, oh yes, she thought dazedly. Higher, harder. She clamped her knees together to strengthen the pressure.

Reese growled against her lips as his entire body

bucked up. Confusion washed over her as she suddenly found herself shoved half a foot away.

Jillian's heart was still racing so fast, she could barely think, much less comprehend what in the world had just happened. She heard Reese's harsh breathing, but couldn't make him out in the darkness. Automatically, she began groping for the lantern. Her sweeping arm smacked against warm, hard denim.

Reese hissed on a sharp intake of breath. "Bloody hell, stay still!"

Jillian froze. Heat of an entirely different sort flooded through her. My God, what had she been thinking? She'd thrown herself at the man. Practically demanded that he pleasure her, for mercy's sake. Oh, dear Lord. Not even when she'd walked into the small apartment she was to share with her future husband, Thomas, only to find her mother standing in the center of the now-empty rooms with a false smile of compassion on her face and her checkbook in her hands had Jillian felt this humiliated.

She could blame it on the storm, on her nerves, on her overwhelming reaction to being cooped up in such a small place with Reese Braedon. Brash, bold, blond, and sexy. Every woman's fantasy come to life. But it wouldn't wash.

Maybe the story she'd overheard Richard regaling her coworkers with on the Valdez expedition had been more painfully correct than she'd been able to admit. Maybe she *was* a frustrated, insecure little wallflower who couldn't hold a man without a checkbook of her own. An attractive man walks into her life and less than three hours later she was flinging herself at him. How much more pathetic could she get?

A sudden blinding light filled the room. Jillian ducked her head instinctively, shielding her eyes from the yellow glow. And from Reese's all-too-perceptive scrutiny.

She was successful only at the former.

"I think—" He broke off on a wince as he shifted his leg. "I think I'll take that painkiller now."

Jillian wanted to get a small spade and start digging. If she was lucky, she'd hit China before she died of mortification. She'd been so carried away, she'd forgotten about his wounded leg. Hot, incredibly clear flashbacks sprang up to torture her. Her hands groping his shoulders, her hips squirming closer, forcing his knee between her legs . . . clamping her thighs around his.

"I'm so sorry," she said on a ragged whisper. She turned and started rummaging through the stacks of boxes, purposely not giving him the chance to reply, certain whatever he said right now would only make matters worse.

She wished with all her might she could turn the light off again. She felt his gaze on her. Imagining what must be going through his mind right now, it was all she could do not to cringe.

She found the box with the medication she was

looking for and slid it over closer to the light, careful to keep her face averted. She hated being such a coward, especially in front of Reese. But she'd had damn good reasons for adopting the lifestyle she had, and this interlude had merely proved her instincts were right. If she was really, really lucky, Reese would be a gentleman and pretend the whole scene had never happened.

"You gonna tell me why you got your head stuck in that box like there was a cure for cancer buried in there somewhere?"

As usual, luck was taking its circuitous route around her. Suddenly weary of the whole thing, she sighed and lifted her head. If they survived the next twenty-four hours, he'd be gone shortly after. If they didn't . . . Well, either way, his opinion of her didn't amount to squat in the overall scheme of things. And the sooner she got that straight in her head the better off she'd be.

She looked at him and extended the medicine bottle, proud of the steadiness of her hand. "Here, take two of these while I get you some water."

He didn't say anything, but held her gaze in a way that made her distinctly uneasy as he reached out to grab the bottle. She should have gone with her instincts. Instead of taking the bottle, he grabbed her wrist and pulled her toward him. His size and strength made the maneuver ridiculously easy. He sat upright, keeping her wrist pinned next to his hip while he used his free hand to tilt up her chin.

Jillian used every scrap of will she had to keep from yanking out of his grasp and scurrying backward like an awkward crab to escape his touch. But nothing short of asphyxiation would keep her from trembling under his touch. Considering that she was finding it equally impossible to breathe, that solution held definite merit.

"You've got this survivor thing down to a science, don't you, mite?"

Her heart pounded under his direct, unreadable expression. Why was he doing this to her? He had to know now how woefully unprepared she was for a man like him. She parted her lips, not sure if it was to breathe or speak but found it didn't matter, since she could do neither.

"I know all about surviving." He tugged gently on her wrist until she bent forward so her weight was braced on both her hands and knees, the motion bringing her perilously close to his mouth again. "But we gotta make a decision, and I'm not sure I'm thinking clearly enough to make the right one."

"About what?" The words were more mouthed than spoken.

"About whether we're going to remember all the reasons we became survivors in the first place." He leaned closer, tilting his head as if he meant to kiss her, but stopping just short of doing so. "Or say to hell with it all and finish what we began a few minutes ago."

SEVEN

If anyone had told Reese yesterday that he would pose a question like that to a small-breasted, diminutive mite with a shade less than zero experience in seducing men—and actually be in pain over her response—he'd have thought the bloke had gone starkers.

The only one starkers here apparently was him. Worse even, he didn't care.

Jillian's eyes were so expressive. Every thought that filtered through her brain was broadcast loud and clear from them. How could he have ever thought them plain? And her breasts might be small, but God, he bet they tasted twice as sweet. His hands nearly spanned her waist, and she'd already proven just how strong her slim thighs were.

He felt his heart rate pick up as he willed her to answer him. One tug against him and he knew he could have her.

But for some reason that wouldn't do. Maybe it was those questions he saw so clearly in her eyes; the doubts, the vulnerability, the survivor in her screaming not to invite him in, not to invite pain. Maybe that was why it had to be her decision.

All he knew was she better make it and damn quick.

"Maybe pleasure isn't enough after all," she whispered finally.

Reese was stunned by the sense of loss, the immediate urge to force a different answer from her. What in the hell was happening to him?

He dropped his hand and shifted away from her. The space he put between them was small, but as effective as the Great Barrier Reef in distancing himself from her. Mentally anyway. His body was registering a very insistent complaint. He ignored it. Discomfort helped him to remain focused.

At least, it always had in the past.

"Reese—"

He looked at her, steeling himself against the possibility that he might see an apology in her expression, or worse yet, pity. No way could he handle that from her. Keeping his expression intentionally shuttered, he was only partially relieved to see that she was doing the same. Or at least trying to. She was just too damn easy to read.

He wondered how many times that had gotten her into trouble. How many times she'd been used, hurt because her emotions and thoughts were on display for anyone with a little calculation and fewer morals to pick up on and use against her.

And how in the bloody hell had she managed to survive it all and still not have learned to shield herself?

"Can you pass me some of the water?" He lifted the medicine bottle to indicate what he wanted it for.

His hard look had prevented her from finishing whatever she'd been about to say. She silently turned to the water jug closest to her, uncapped it, then slid it across the floor toward him.

"Here. You might not want to drink too much—"

"I know we need to conserve water."

"I wasn't thinking of that so much as . . ." Her voice trailed off, and the most becoming pink color bloomed on cheeks that had gone pale the moment he'd made his proposition.

"Nature's call," he finished. "Good point." He tossed the pills down without benefit of water. He hadn't needed any in the first place, had asked only because it had been the most efficient way to shut her up. "Here." He slid the bottle back to her. "Better recap it."

She did and carefully positioned it where it had been, as if the entire structure of the room hinged on her getting it in exactly the right spot.

"Jillian."

She stilled, but didn't turn toward him.

Damn. Why were things so difficult with her?

"Maybe we should talk about what we might be facing in the next few hours. Come up with some plans in case . . ." She turned to face him. "You know, in case things don't go smoothly."

"You mean in case one of us gets hurt? Or dies?" She crossed her legs and shifted to fully face him. "Just because I'm not comfortable with intimacy doesn't mean I can't handle reality. Don't tiptoe around me."

"Strange, that."

"What do you mean?"

"That life and death issues are easier to handle than personal ones."

"You say that as if you're not just talking about me."

"Does that surprise you?"

"Maybe. A little."

"What, I look like a man who wears his emotions on his sleeve?"

She snorted. It wasn't a ladylike sound. It made him want to laugh. It also made him more determined than ever to taste her again. Taste her smiles, her laughter. Her—

"It's just that you seem very comfortable with your body. You're in tune with its needs and demands."

That got his full attention. He didn't dare react. Did she have any idea she was handling explosives here?

"Knowing how to satisfy my sexual needs and

being intimate are two different things." He could hardly believe he'd said that. Admitted that.

"I suppose you're right," she said thoughtfully.

"What, you don't know?" He leaned in her direction. "Have you never just satisfied your body and not your mind?" He did it all the time. Every time, if the truth be told.

He noticed the stiffness creep into her spine and shoulders, the way her hands clutched at each other as she tucked her knees under her chin in the ultimate defensive posture. But her gaze remained hard on his, her expression making it clear she'd taken his question like a challenge. One she apparently intended to meet. But with obvious cost.

"I think I've always been so concerned with fulfilling the sexual needs of . . . of my . . . partner that, well, I've never really thought about mine."

Oh, mite, he thought, what a waste. He started to speak but she went on, apparently needing to get it all out.

"As for intimacy, yes, I think I've had that."

She thought? Well hell, he wasn't exactly an expert on the subject himself. Except to know when there wasn't any.

"At least, I've wanted it. I mean, I've never had casual sex. Just for the . . ."

"Release? Orgasm?"

She looked taken aback by his harsh intrusion.

"No tiptoeing, remember?"

Her eyes narrowed. *Yeah*, he thought, *there's my battler*.

"Yes. And the answer is no. I've never had sex just for the orgasm."

Her color heightened. In another woman, Reese would have read it as anger or defiance. And those emotions were present. But so was fear. Fear of discovery.

She'd never had an orgasm. He'd bet every one he'd ever had—every one he'd ever given—on it.

He thought back over his life and all the times he'd been with a woman. Take away the physical climax and what did he have left? Not much. Maybe nothing. Jillian had said she'd wanted intimacy in her relationships, but Reese doubted she'd found even that. So what had she gotten?

Less than nothing.

The realization hit him like a hard punch to the gut. Air suddenly became a precious commodity. His need for her had just gone from necessary to imperative. Not because he wanted to play macho stud and teach the little sexual ingenue about peaking in all its wonderful variations—though he wouldn't deny the idea of awakening her turned him on in ways he'd never dreamed. No, he wanted her because the very idea of Jillian looking into the eyes of another man the first time she hit that crest was simply untenable.

And yet he wouldn't be the one. Couldn't be.

The revelation itself had been too powerful. Too stunning. Too potent. And he had a very disturbing notion that the price for being the one would be intimacy.

Even if he wanted to—and he didn't want to contemplate that he might—it was a price he couldn't pay.

Worse, it was a price he wasn't certain he was capable of paying. His childhood had seen to that. And the years spent cleaning up the back streets of Miami certainly hadn't changed it any.

And Jillian, with all her ghosts, and her battles so hard won and so painfully lost, deserved nothing less.

"Good on you, then," he said at last. "You're the lucky one." He shifted slightly, hoping to ease the persistent ache between his legs, and forced his thoughts back to their more immediate problems.

He never had the chance.

A tremendous boom rocked the house, followed by horrific tearing sounds, as if the house was being rent in two like a piece of fabric. The noise became so loud, it hurt his ears. "Get near the middle stack of boxes!" Reese yelled as loud as he could. He reached for the edges of the mattress and yanked until one whole side caved in, then scooted around to the next side. Jillian saw what he was up to and moved to the edge nearest her and began to tug.

Reese's first instinct was to order her back to the relative safety of the center of the room, but there was no time for arguing.

In minutes that seemed like years, they had pulled down all four sides of the heavy mattress to blanket them, with only a small stack in the center to lift the mattress and provide breathing space.

Reese reached out and pulled Jillian back against him. "Stay down, close to the boxes."

He'd intended for her to curl up close to the center stack so he could curve his body around her, shielding her the best he could. Instead she turned to face him.

The screeching wail and moan of the wind made it difficult for him to hear what she was saying.

"What happened? Is the house collapsing on us?"

He pulled her against his chest and pushed her face into the crook of his neck, turning his head so his mouth was level with her ear. "Part of it's gone. That's why the sound is so much louder."

She leaned up, her lips grazing his earlobe. Despite the adrenaline pounding throughout his system—or maybe because of it—his body leapt in response. Damn, she was so soft and sweet. And strong. And tough.

"What do you think our chances are, Reese?"

He pulled his head back, trying to look into her eyes. It was too dark. Any other woman would be falling apart, screaming, going starkers on him. Not Jillian.

She held him tightly, her body trembled, but her question demanded an honest answer. He gave her one.

"Not the best."

He felt her still for a second, then let her head

rest once again beside his neck. The action was simple, and yet so very complex. She trusted him.

And he'd never in his life wanted to be worthy of a person's trust like he did right then.

He let his hands drift up and down her back, tucked her legs in closer to his, the wound on his thigh the least of his concerns at this point.

"Reese?"

He bent his head closer to her lips. "Mmmmm?"

"Thank you."

He pulled his head away in a sharp movement, looking down at her. "What in the hell for?"

She must have heard him, because she tugged him closer and spoke into his ear. "I know you were just doing your job, but I'm glad I'm not going through this alone. I'm sorry you're here because of me."

An ache formed in the center of his chest. Damn, here they were about to get done in by Ivan, and *she* was reassuring *him*. Apologizing.

"If I'd done my job, neither of us would be here. Don't apologize," he said gruffly. He wondered if he should tell her who had actually sent him here. If they weren't going to make it, maybe it would bring her some peace to know that her mother cared enough about her to try and protect her.

He wished now he knew more of the history between them. He thought again of the photo tucked inside the trash bag, stashed somewhere in the small room where they were huddled.

"Talk to me, Jillian. Take our minds off the storm." He pulled her closer to him. She moved willingly and he discovered that it bothered him a great deal not to know whether she'd have done the same without the dire threat of the storm hanging over their heads.

Had another man been hired in his place, would she be in his arms right now?

He was the one going crazy now. And yet he couldn't ignore the fierce gladness he felt that it was him, not any other man.

"I'm worried about Cleo," she said, breaking into his erratic thoughts.

"Alligators survive hurricanes. She could be all right."

"She'll lose her nestlings."

He let his hand drift into her hair, running his fingers through the short length over and over. "She can have more, can't she?"

"Hard to say. She gets around okay with three legs. But I can't know for certain she will mate again."

He felt her sigh against him.

"Was there something special about these particular eggs, Jillian?" He wasn't sure why he'd asked, just an instinct.

"Not really. At least, not to anyone else." A light shudder passed through her slender body.

"Oh, Reese," she sighed, the words coming out all wobbly.

She was going to cry now? After all that had happened and she was going to cry over some silly eggs? But they weren't silly to her.

"Why are they special to you?" he asked gently.

"She struggled so hard to survive. I really thought I wasn't going to be able to save her. And then I found out she was pregnant and . . ."

"What?"

"I just couldn't shake the feeling that she'd pushed so hard so she could lay her eggs."

"That's not all that unnatural, is it? I mean, most animals' driving force is to reproduce, right?"

There was a long pause. "Yes, it is." Her voice had dropped a level or two. It pulled at Reese, making him want to ask her crazy things. Like if she'd ever wanted children. She'd make a great mom, he thought. Better than her own, probably. Certainly better than his. He'd never even let himself think about having a family. His own had been a nightmare of neglect while he watched his parents' dreams slowly corrode away. A family of his own was a dream he'd never be able to do justice to, so there was no use torturing himself over it.

"I helped her lay the eggs," Jillian said at length.

"You what?" he demanded. "Was she sedated or something?" So help him, if she said no—

"No, she—"

He gripped her shoulders. "What in the hell

were you doing? You'd be nothing more than a snack to her. And don't give me any crap about you taming her. You told me you were planning on releasing her and you'd never do that if she'd been anything less than the predator she was born to be."

Jillian had stiffened in his arms. He wondered for a half second if she would pull away. He didn't even think about what his automatic response may have revealed about the way he felt about her.

Whoa. How did he feel about her?

His grip tightened. He wasn't sure. But he did know that for the duration of the storm she wasn't going to put so much as an inch between them. For now, that would be enough. He'd examine the rest later. If there was a later.

"When alligators lay their eggs, they are completely focused on it. No outside intrusion breaks in. Normally, I wouldn't have interfered, but she was having trouble balancing and I was afraid she'd squash the eggs as they came out. So I helped prop her up so they would drop into the nest."

Reese let out a deep breath. "Lady, you're crazy." He squeezed her in a short, tight hug. "But the animals are sure as hell lucky to have you on their side."

"So you understand why I had to stay?"

There was such hope in her voice, he hated to deflate it. "Not really, Jillian. I know why she's special to you, but—"

"I'd made a commitment to her, Reese. More of

one than I've made in a long, long time. I couldn't move her. And I couldn't leave her."

Reese lifted her chin, staring down at her in the dark. "Your life is worth so much. Why risk it for one animal?"

"The same reason you're here. It's my job."

It was a hell of a lot more than that, he knew. But he also heard the defensiveness in her voice, the dismissal. Whatever reason she'd had for confiding in him had disappeared. But she made no move to leave the shelter of his arms, and he forced himself to be content with that.

For several long minutes they remained silent, the ominous sounds of the storm raged around them. Reese tried to blank his mind and focus on anything other than the woman in his arms and all the conflicting emotions she'd dredged up in him.

"What about you, Reese?"

No, was his immediate response. Absolutely not. He'd made it a habit never to talk about himself. But this denial went deeper. Some part of him knew that Jillian Bonner was a threat. A threat to his privacy? Definitely. A threat to his innermost boundaries? The ones that kept the entire world at a safe, impersonal distance? A distance that made his job easier? Maybe even one that guaranteed he'd never end up like his parents?

Oh yeah.

And the very idea that he'd let her get close enough to even be considered a threat rocked him to his very core.

"What do you want to know?" he asked, his voice rough with the effort to sound casual.

"Tell me about Australia." She ducked her head slightly. "I think I could listen to you talk for hours," she added shyly.

His chest tightened, and the ache that was centered lower and deeper inside him grew. "Hours? You'll be disappointed then."

"The strong, silent type, huh?"

Her teasing tone did amazing things to his pulse rate.

"Not much to talk about."

"What part of Australia are you from? Surely you can part with that much of yourself."

Her perception shook him up a bit. And he had the oddest urge to tell her whatever she wanted to know. Tempted, for the first time since childhood, to share something of himself, to risk giving a piece of himself away. To her.

Dangerous thoughts. And it was precisely that sort of danger he'd avoided by avoiding intimacy on anything but the basest level. Physical. Primal.

Not mental. Never emotional.

"Western Australia in a place called Broome. It's a pearling town on the northwest coast."

"Pearls? That's pretty tough work, isn't it?"

Reese smiled. "Most women would be in rapture over the romantic aspects of pearls. You only see the hard, rough side."

"Yes, well, most beautiful things come from ugly, harsh beginnings."

Reese placed his hands on her face and lifted it to his. "Like you, mite?"

"I'm hardly beautiful."

"On the contrary, I think you're the most truly beautiful person I've ever met."

"Reese, don't—"

"Shhh." He ducked his head and did what he'd been wanting to do almost since the instant their lips had parted. It seemed like centuries ago.

A groan surged into his throat as he took her mouth. Damn she was sweet and sensual in ways he'd never dreamed a woman could be. Never had he wanted someone so strongly, felt the need to bury himself inside a woman so desperately. It was as if there was far more to be joined than just their bodies.

It was a connection so unique, so tantalizing he couldn't resist going after it.

He slanted his mouth across hers and took the kiss deeper. His hands framing her face gentled, and he let his fingers plunge into her hair, then drop down to her shoulders.

He felt the trembling in her, felt her grab at his shoulders as if she were hanging on for dear life. And yet he couldn't stop, didn't want to know she might not be feeling what he was feeling. What he'd never felt before.

He slid his tongue into her mouth, filling it, tasting her, wanting more. So much more.

She moaned and moved against him in a way

that removed all doubt from his mind. She was with him. Body, mind, soul. And spirit.

What a tremendous spirit she had. Her tongue dueled with his, demanding entry into his mouth where she ravaged him as he'd ravaged her. She wanted, she took.

He capitulated willingly, stunned by how deeply her needs moved him, motivated him to give her whatever she sought, praying like hell he had it to give.

He pulled her under him, rolling half on top of her in the small, cramped space provided by the short stack of boxes. He continued to duel with her mouth, taking turns controlling the kisses they were sharing.

He slid his hands from her shoulders to her waist, pulled her up against him, needing some contact between the softness of her and the hardness of him. And dear God had he ever been this hard? His big hands covered her stomach, and he lifted himself enough to pull her shirt from the waistband of her jeans.

Her arms were twined around his neck, urging him not to break the delicious contact of their hungry lips. He struggled to comply. She was so much smaller than him, it was hard to bend his body to reach all the places he wanted to reach.

He finally broke off the kiss, needing to explore the rest of her. She groaned her disapproval, then sucked in a sharp breath when he pushed her shirt up.

"Reese." The whisper was harsh. She stiffened.

He scooted down so his face was even with her torso and dropped his head to kiss her flat stomach. "Let me, Jillian."

"But I'm—" Her words were cut off on a gasp as he bared her breasts.

"Shhh." More than anything in the world Reese wished they'd left the battery lantern on. But he was too caught up in his discovery of her to search for it now.

His hands moved up and covered her breasts completely. Jillian squirmed under his touch. "Mmmmm," Reese groaned. "Exquisite."

"There's . . ." She broke off as he started a light massage. "Not much there," she finished on a gasp.

"Maybe not," he answered, tweaking her nipples gently into even tauter peaks. "But it's like pearls; it's not always the size, but the perfection." He dipped his head and took one of her nipples into his mouth, then moved to the other one. On a soft groan he laid his head between her breasts. "And I'd say these are top quality."

She'd stiffened under his gentle assault, even as she moaned and writhed. Only now did she relax under him. When he felt her hands tentatively touch his hair, then move more assuredly against his scalp, he sighed deeply.

This was far from the first time his head had been pillowed between a woman's breasts. So why did it feel so different?

He moved his head to nuzzle her again, slowly laving each nipple, reveling in the way she arched against him more naturally this time. He knew she'd be so easy to bring to a peak, her body was fairly screaming for it.

Not that he could blame it. If he'd gone without ever climaxing, he'd have probably picked it a long time ago.

Each and every muscle in his body tensed as he contemplated moving his attention slowly southward. A million sensations rushed through him at the merest idea of how she'd respond under his lips, his tongue.

"Reese." Her tone was urgent, demanding. Reese understood.

"I know, sweetheart, I know." He shifted, spreading light kisses along the center of her stomach, lingering over her navel, finding the whole experience of discovering her in the dark both frustrating and immensely erotic. He unsnapped her jeans quietly, and began to pull on the zipper.

"Reese." Her voice was rougher, deeper, but this time she leaned up and reached down for his shoulders, tugging at him. "Come back up here."

Reese experienced a moment of deep indecision. Everything in him was urging him to continue on the path he'd begun. She hadn't tensed under him—at least not in a negative way—and she didn't seem to be panicking now. Far from it. Her body felt soft and languid beneath him.

"Please."

Sighing softly against her still-zipped jeans, he carefully shifted upward, not pulling her shirt down, but wishing like hell his was off so he could feel her bare breasts against his chest. He vowed then and there that he would. Sometime. Somehow.

Shifting carefully to his side, favoring his sore thigh, he pulled her to him, bending his head down to hers. "What is it, Jillian? Was I going too fast?"

"No."

He smiled again, suddenly not minding that they'd slowed down a bit. "You sound surprised."

"I guess I am. Reese, I . . ." She ducked her head, resting her forehead on his shoulder for a moment.

He lifted her face to his with a finger beneath her chin. "You've never made love with a man during a hurricane?" He kept his tone carefully light, completely ignoring the fact that he'd called what they'd been doing lovemaking, when he'd never referred to it as anything but sex before.

"That's true. And I didn't want you to stop. Not really."

"Then why did you?"

"Because I'm not . . . that is, I don't use . . . anything. And I didn't think you . . ." She buried her head again. "Dear Lord," she muttered against his chest, "I'm over thirty, I'm not a virgin. You'd think I could talk about birth control without stammering."

Reese actually felt his heart swell in his chest.

She was strong and tough, and wonderfully adorable in ways he wouldn't have imagined he'd enjoy in a woman. "I would have stopped." He lifted a quick finger to her lips when he felt her tense as if to speak. "I wouldn't have liked it, but I would have stopped." He leaned down and gave her a hard, fast kiss. Because he thought she needed the reassurance, and because he damn well wanted to. Then he whispered against her mouth, "But if I were you, I would have waited about five more minutes. You'd be feeling a lot better now than you do."

She punched him lightly on the shoulder.

"What? It's the truth."

"Pretty sure of yourself, aren't you?"

In his best Southern American drawl, he said, "Why yes, ma'am, I am."

She hugged him tightly, and he hugged her right back. Damn but he didn't think he ever wanted the storm to end. It would mean he'd have to let her go. And he was beginning to realize that it was going to be more difficult than he'd ever thought possible.

"Reese?"

"Yes?"

"Does this mean we have to stop kissing?"

His body answered with a resounding no. "Nah. I imagine it would irritate old Ivan to death out there if he knew how much fun we were havin' while he was doing his darnedest to wreak havoc."

"Can I . . . would you . . . ?"

"You're cute when you stammer."

She thumped him on the chest. "I take it back. I liked you better when you let your actions speak for you." Without another word, she reached down and tugged his shirt up.

"Well, never let it be said that I disappointed a lady." He ripped off his shirt and quickly settled his mouth back on hers. Shifting to his back, he pulled her half on top of him, groaning deeply at the feel of her small breasts rubbing along his rib cage. "Damn you feel good."

"You too, Reese. You too."

EIGHT

Jillian woke up slowly. Awareness filtered in in fragments, like pieces of a kaleidoscope falling into place. Memories of Reese kissing her, of her kissing Reese, of her heart pounding and feeling Reese's pulse race under her lips when she kissed his neck. His hands on her, her hands on him . . . She remembered Reese slowing things down by getting her to talk, teasing her into recounting stories both funny and sad about her travails as a wildlife rehabilitator.

And at some indefinable point along the way, she'd fallen asleep. Or had she?

Her eyes flew open as it occurred to her what had woken her up. If in fact she could be woken up. The noise. Or more to the point, the total lack of it.

She couldn't see a thing. But she felt a heavy weight pressing against her chest and abdomen.

"Are we dead?" she whispered, then felt disappointed when the question didn't sound as absurd spoken outloud as she'd hoped it would.

"God, I hope not," came a raspy reply.

Reese shifted his head, and the bristle of his beard scraped against her left breast. Her bare left breast.

Before she could react, he turned his head and pulled her nipple into his mouth, having no problem locating it even without a bit of light. As if he'd reached for it before.

More than once.

She arched automatically under his touch as a dozen sensations warred with twice as many questions for her immediate attention. It was a toss-up as to which side was winning the battle, but when he shifted his attention to her other breast things slanted swiftly toward the sensations' side.

"Reese," she gasped. Something niggled at the back of her brain . . . something that had caught her attention, woken her up. What he was doing felt so good. But . . .

Suddenly she reached down and shoved at his shoulders and head. "Reese, stop."

"Don't wanna," he mumbled against her soft skin. "Let me enjoy heaven before someone figures out they made a mistake and sent me in the wrong direction."

"The storm, Reese, the storm. Listen!"

With a groan and deep heartfelt sigh that oddly enough made her mouth curl in the beginnings of a smile, he lifted his head. After a silent moment, he said, "It's over."

Jillian wanted to believe that almost as much as she wished Reese would go back to what he'd just been doing. She shook off the last vestiges of the seductive drowsiness of her waking moments.

"How do you know it's not just the eye passing over us?" she asked, listening hard for any signs that the storm still raged. She heard nothing.

"Been too long. It's over."

"We made it?" She whispered the question, as if afraid Ivan was still hovering outside and might overhear that he'd unknowingly left a survivor or two.

"Yeah, mite. We made it."

Her thoughts instantly shifted to Cleo. Had she survived as well? Jillian immediately began to struggle to crawl out from under Reese. Her progress was stopped short when he pinned her back down with strong hands on her shoulders.

"Hold on there a minute." He slid off of her. "Let me make sure the only thing on top of us is this mattress."

She heard him shuffle a bit, then, remembering her state of dress—or rather, undress—she quietly pulled down her shirt. She tried not to let herself think about the sudden sense of loss that flooded her as she realized her time with Reese was probably over. Not that they'd done anything earth-shattering that would have permanent repercussions.

Unless you called spending twelve hours in the arms of the most tantalizing man she'd ever met earth-shattering.

"Feels sound," he said a minute later. "I'm gonna prop this side back up, you feel around over there for a battery lantern."

Jillian willingly shoved aside her seesawing emotions and did as Reese asked.

"I've got to check on Cleo. Right away." She found the lantern and switched it on, then swung her forearm over her eyes as the unnatural brightness filled the small space.

When she'd adjusted, she peered at Reese, whose eyes were also squinched up.

"Takes a bit of getting used to. Feel like a mole."

"I know what you mean," she replied, finally lowering her arm completely. "Is it day or night outside?"

Reese glanced at the watch on his wrist, taking a moment to focus on the small dial. "Morning. A bit past seven."

"Good, at least we'll be able to see the damage outside."

"Jillian," he began, his tone one of warning.

She held up her hand. "I know. At least, I know that it may be horrible. I don't imagine I could possibly really prepare myself. Except I keep thinking of the scenes after Andrew." She shuddered and rubbed her arms. "It'll be different since it's . . . my home . . . that's rubble."

"You're alive, Jillian."

Her gaze connected with his. Damn but he looked as good and strong and reassuring as he'd felt all through the long, dark hours of the night. "Yes, you're right. Thank you, Reese."

"Don't thank me, thank Ivan."

Ivan didn't hold me for the last twelve hours. "If I'd spent last night alone, I'd have fallen apart long ago. That is if I'd been able to protect myself in here as well as you did."

Reese stared at her for a few moments, his expression unreadable. Then he said, "You wouldn't have fallen apart. You're strong, Jillian Bonner. You do what has to be done."

He continued to stare, and Jillian got the uneasy feeling he was distancing himself from her, like he was cataloging her, storing his time with her away. There was no deeper, more personal message lurking in his flat eyes. Nothing to indicate he'd spent the better part of the last twelve hours with his face between her breasts, or with his lips fastened on hers.

She swallowed her regret, determined to take this next step in stride without embarrassing either one of them. Maybe it was just as well they pulled back now, she told herself. She'd need all her strength and concentration to deal with what she was likely to find on the other side of the closet door.

Their parting was inevitable, anyway.

They'd come together in a crisis, when the line

between life and death had thinned to almost invisible proportions. She was not stupid enough to think that what they had shared in the darkness would survive in the light.

It was as simple as that. Painful, but expected.

She squared her shoulders. "That may or may not be true," she answered him at length. "But the fact remains that you *were* here and I'll always be grateful to you for that."

Without waiting for his reply, she rolled onto her hands and knees and went about pushing her side of the mattress back up onto the boxes. Once that was done she faced Reese again, careful to keep her demeanor and tone businesslike.

"What's the best way of getting out of here? I don't want to move something, or open the door, and have the remainder of the house cave in on our heads."

"Slowly. First, let's get this mattress folded under so we can stand up. Scoot over here next to me and help me shove this half onto the other side."

Jillian did as he'd asked, but paid a price for being so close to him again. She could smell him, even the heat of his body made her pulse pound, and she had to quickly duck her head before he looked up and caught what she knew was written plainly on her face.

She still wanted him. She wanted to finish what she hadn't let him really start last night. And she wanted it so bad, she hurt.

And they said pain was a great teacher. Well, if that was the case, she should be a scholar.

What she felt like was the class dunce.

They made short work of the mattress. She stood and immediately began to massage the sudden cramping that assaulted her thighs and calves as her blood flow obeyed the force of gravity.

Out of the corner of her eye she caught Reese wince and hop a bit off to one side before catching his balance with a hand on the wall.

She'd forgotten. "Your leg. Let me look at it."

"It's okay. Just cramped a bit when I stood." He turned. "Let me check the door."

Jillian watched him lift the lantern and examine the doorframe, she assumed for cracks or stress fractures. She didn't pursue checking his wound, telling herself he was a grown man and could look after himself. It was easier and less shaming than admitting the very last thing she wanted to do was come in to close contact with his bare skin—no matter what the reason.

Reese angled the light at the ceiling. "Looks sound from in here." He turned and twisted the doorknob slowly, then opened the door a crack. Nothing crashed down or caved in. He turned to face her. "You ready?"

"As I'll ever be." She took a deep breath and moved to the door. She reached past him to grab the knob.

"Jillian." His voice was low, husky. Private. Without the background noise of the storm, his rich accent filled her name with mysterious texture. It sounded almost . . . intimate.

Jillian realized then that she didn't want to hear any emotion in his voice. Flat and distanced was better, made it easier for her to remain focused. She bowed her head for a brief moment, then looked up at him. "It's okay, Reese," she said quietly. "Really. I've got to check on Cleo."

"Right." The distance was back. He moved away.

Shoulders squared, mind carefully blank, Jillian opened the door and stepped out into the hallway.

Behind her she heard Reese whisper, "Good on you, mite. Good on you."

The respect she heard in his voice was the only thing that carried her through the next several seconds without buckling to the ground.

Her hand rose slowly to cover her open mouth. In the next instant, Reese's strong hands covered her shoulders and pulled her stiffened body back against his.

The kitchen still stood, but her office was rubble. It looked as if the corner of the house had been accidentally stepped on by a huge giant whose long stride hadn't quite cleared the width of the house. She twisted from Reese's hold and looked behind him, back down the hall toward the front door. It looked fine. Except for the unnatural amount of light streaming down the staircase.

She took two steps in that direction, but Reese stopped her, his hand on her arm.

"Let me." He moved in front of her before she could answer.

A step behind him, she spotted the rubble at the base of the stairs only a second after he did. She slowly raised her gaze upward, up the staircase now littered with remains of what had been the upper level of her house.

"Dear God," she breathed, in complete awe, truly aware for the first time the enormity of the danger they'd been in. She'd known what she was risking, or thought she had. But this . . . this . . . destruction, so casually ripping apart a piece of her life here, then generously sparing another, as if on some evil-minded whim.

Reese grasped her shoulders and turned her back toward the kitchen. "We can't check the front bedroom, too much rubble piled at the bottom. Let's get out of here. Until we see the extent of the damage from the outside, we don't know where it's safe to be."

Jillian stretched her head back and took one last glimpse up the stairs. There was so much structural garbage blocking the entrance to the upper hall, it was hard to tell how much of the roof had caved in. But the amount of light streaming in and around the mess up there made it a certainty that at least part of it was gone.

"Let's check on Cleo." He gently prodded her forward.

Like a zombie, she took two steps forward, then swung around, and buried her head on Reese's shoulder. His arms came around her immediately, holding her tightly against his chest.

"You're alive, Jillian, you're alive," he whispered, his warm lips nuzzling her ear. "Nothing else matters."

Jillian's eyes burned but no tears would come. She wondered absently if she was going into shock. She concentrated on the steady beat of Reese's heart under her cheek, and forced her breathing into the same even cadence. In, out. In, out. She'd be okay, she'd be okay.

They were alive. Reese was right, nothing else mattered.

"So why does it feel as if my life has come to an end anyway?" She hadn't been aware of speaking out loud until Reese answered.

"We'll make it right again, Jillian. It'll take more than a passing fair amount of time, but we'll make it right."

She barely heard him. The enormity and strength, the sheer magnitude of the storm to have done damage like this . . .

Cleo. The thought jumped into the jumble her mind had become. Her head shot up. "I've got to check on Cleo. Or"—she pushed out of Reese's arms with a sudden burst of energy and determination, her brain racing forward—"maybe you should do a perimeter check while I go find out how she is."

"I'll go with you."

"It's okay," she rushed on, turning toward the kitchen. "I'm fine really, I'll be—"

She didn't have a chance to finish. Reese simply took her hand in his, slipped his fingers between hers and began picking his way over the rubble that had blown into the kitchen from the destruction that had once been her office. "Watch your step."

Jillian looked down automatically, then froze when she saw what she'd been about to step over. After a split second she stooped down and grabbed the carved wooden lamp that just yesterday had been on the nightstand in her bedroom.

She turned it over. The lamp shade was gone and bulb fixture mangled, but the twin dolphins still arced gracefully out of a beautifully carved wave, the smiles on their faces a silent mocking to Ivan and the havoc he'd wrought.

The world slowly rocked back to center. Jillian carefully filtered out all the myriad things beckoning her attention. There would be time later to sort out the long-term effects of the devastation the storm had left behind.

She set the lamp carefully on the kitchen table, which had been left untouched by the storm. And, without wanting to, she tightened her hold on Reese's hand. Right that minute it felt like a lifeline, and she wasn't too proud to admit that she could use one.

"Help me get the bars off the door, okay?"

Jillian was grateful for the task, to do even the smallest chore meant she was moving forward, that the worst was over and every step, no matter how tiny, was a step away from this . . . this . . .

She shuddered lightly, but dropped Reese's hand. "Okay. Do you want to get the mop handle from the storage room for a crutch?"

"Nah. Not that bad, really. I guess the enforced rest of last night was good for something."

She didn't even want to think about last night. Couldn't, if she wanted to retain what small part of her control she'd won back.

But she watched him out of the corner of her eye as he stepped to his side of the door. He limped, favoring his wounded thigh more than a little, but he could walk. She turned her attention back to the door, and what lay beyond it. Or rather who. Cleo.

"Let me push, then you pull," he directed. "The door seems to have warped a bit."

Five minutes and a few swear words later the door swung open.

"The porch is gone," she said, stating the obvious. Her mind registered the incredible amount of garbage, both natural and man-made, strewn about the grounds of the compound. But most of her attention was focused on one small part. The pond.

She looked down for a safe place to jump, as without the benefit of the porch, she'd also lost the stairs. Reese levered himself down first and motioned her to follow him.

Once on the ground, she passed Reese on her way toward the pond. "At least there's no flooding," she called over her shoulder, realizing it felt strange not to have to yell to be heard. She scanned the grounds. Downed trees and limbs and what was probably chunks of her roof blocked her line of vision. She headed in what appeared to be the most direct route around it.

A small crash and a string of colorful cursing made her slow down enough to look over her shoulder.

Reese was bent over holding his shin, but he motioned her on. "Go on, I'll catch up."

Jillian nodded, using all of her concentration not to look past Reese at her house—or what was left of it—and turned her attention back on picking out her path. Not now, she said silently. Cleo first, then the house. The house wasn't going anywhere. At least not what was left of it.

Her thoughts flipped to the egg mound as she wondered about the nestlings' fate. A waterlogged egg mound would be fatal for the soon-to-be hatchlings. A quick glance skyward showed it was still overcast, but the rain and wind had stopped. "Please," she prayed softly, "don't bring more rain." She knew the fact that it hadn't flooded yet didn't mean the threat was past. Caracoles Key was small, and a storm of Ivan's magnitude had likely wreaked its havoc on the tides as well as the island. Her compound was on the eastern side closest to Sanibel, but that didn't insure it against the threat of flooding.

She rounded the last twisted piece of siding and

caught her first good look at the pond . . . and the mound. The pond had swollen past its banks, but it had stopped several feet shy of infiltrating the mound. Cleo, she didn't see Cleo.

Without realizing it, she broke into a run, not stopping until she was halfway around the pond. There she was! Jillian raised her finger, pointing out to no one in particular the dark shadow lying in the shallows at the edge of the pond.

Jillian stopped near the edge of the pond, positioning herself to get the best glance without risking antagonizing Cleo. She had no idea what state Cleo would be in after suffering through such an ordeal, but she had immense respect for the huge reptile and wasn't about to jeopardize herself or the alligator.

But she'd give her soul for a pair of her best binoculars right now. Those particular binoculars had been stored in her office. The reality of the devastation blindsided her, literally taking her breath away for a long, painful moment.

Again, she felt large, warm hands cover her shoulders. "Breathe slowly."

She did, and a moment later he dropped his hands. Jillian wished he hadn't, but didn't say anything. Some protective part of her brain still functioned and knew she could easily begin to rely too heavily on the reassurance Reese had so readily supplied for the last twelve hours.

"Is she all right?"

"I haven't seen her move yet, but she's still near

the mound, and it doesn't look damaged. At least it's not flooded from what I can tell."

"How will you know for sure?"

She tore her gaze away from Cleo and turned to face Reese. Her heart skipped erratically again, as she was also taken off guard by how much she'd come to enjoy looking at him, looking *to* him. "With Cleo, mostly observation. I'll have to get closer if she seems to be suffering. As for the nestlings, we'll know in a couple of days when they're due to hatch. They all hatch at the same time, so it will be easy enough to tell."

"Why did you name her Cleo?"

A wistful smile curved her lips. "It's Cleopatra actually. The Egyptians revered the crocodile family. And she was so . . . I don't know. She deserved a royal name. I thought it suited her."

He didn't respond, instead he simply looked at her, into her.

"What?" she asked finally, unable to handle his scrutiny with her control so thinly stretched.

"You." At her lifted eyebrows, he took a step closer and brought his hand to her face. She let him push errant strands of hair off her forehead and run a rough-tipped finger down her cheek.

"What about me?" His touch was far more soothing than it had a right to be. Her heart warred with her brain over the inherent stupidity of asking him such a loaded question at a time like this.

"I've never met anyone like you. You're strong, you're tough, you're courageous."

"Don't you mean foolish, stupid, and reckless?"

"That too. Except for the stupid part." His mouth tipped up at the corners in a rusty smile. "But that's not bad, for a sheila."

Lord, the man *could* smile. And what a smile it was. What it did for his eyes . . . what it did for the darkness behind those eyes . . . She found herself doing the most ridiculous thing, considering the circumstances. She smiled back.

"And you're not too bad, either. For an Aussie." His smile broadened.

And then she was in his arms and he was kissing her relentlessly. There was no time to breathe, even less time to think.

His kisses were pushing her, driving her, testing her. And still she couldn't think, couldn't determine what else he wanted from her.

Jillian stood in his arms and absorbed the brunt of his passion. His kisses buffeted her mind, body, and soul just as the raging winds had buffeted her house and home. And she was as helpless against the forces of nature driving Reese as she'd been against those driving Ivan. As helpless as she'd been against her mother's determination and scheming, as helpless as she'd been to prevent Thomas from walking away from her and the life she'd expected to share with him, as helpless as she'd been to prevent Richard from taking her private pain and making it so humiliatingly public.

Helpless. As she'd been made to feel all her life.

Something deep inside her clicked. Or maybe it snapped.

And the whirling maelstrom of emotions that she'd learned long ago to keep forcibly locked in a far corner of her mind sprang forth past the old, protective barrier.

Violent, powerful, enervating, the force of it flowed through her, energizing her. Revitalizing her.

And then she was moving in his arms, a compliant receiver no more. She pulled at him, kissed him back, moved her body against his as he had against hers. She didn't think, she didn't wonder, she just acted.

And he liked it.

Jillian knew from his response, from the groans she felt erupting inside his chest, from the hot words of encouragement he broke off to whisper roughly in her ear.

But he wasn't compliant, as she'd been. He continued to take even while he gave, each of them fighting for what they wanted, reveling as much in each other's victories as they did their own.

And suddenly she didn't feel so weak, she didn't feel so victimized. She didn't feel so damn helpless.

No. She felt like the woman he thought her to be. Strong. Tough. Courageous.

And as swiftly as it had swept over her, over them, the storm receded. In unison, their kisses gentled, slowed, until they simply stood in each other's arms, Reese looking down at her, Jillian's gaze fixed on him.

"Thank you," she whispered hoarsely, when she finally could.

His brow lifted, as if to say he didn't understand her meaning. But his eyes betrayed him. Now, in the light of day, Jillian could see what she'd only suspected was there during the long dark night she'd spent in his arms.

Gone were his walls, his defenses, defenses she suspected were as old and as painfully erected as hers had been. Now she could see behind them, into him. And there was pain, and sadness, and wariness.

She felt strangely as if she was looking into a mirror.

But there was also strength, honor, and faith. And a fierceness, a banked sort of heat that had nothing to do with protecting himself. She felt her knees begin to buckle.

Reese's arms tightened around her as if to hold her up. But his expression darkened, and the flickering heat danced in his eyes, threatening to erupt into flames, his steely control the only thing keeping them both from being scorched by what lay behind it. And as her own arms tightened around him in automatic response, she wondered who was supporting whom.

But Jillian knew what she was looking at, even if she'd never seen it before, she knew she was seeing it now. And she suspected he'd seen it too. In her own eyes.

Intimacy. They'd become intimate. Not just physically, barely physically really. They hadn't entered each other's bodies. No, they'd become intimate in a far more dangerous way. They had entered each other's minds.

Each other's souls.

And once breached, that barrier was just as irreversible as any physical one. Possibly more so.

Jillian knew in that moment she couldn't have felt any more open and vulnerable to another man than if he stripped her naked, pulled her down, and drove himself into her right here on the hard, wet ground.

Reese's hands lifted to her face, he cupped her cheeks and bent his head down. "Don't thank me," he whispered, when he was just a breath away. "It's not me, Jillian. It's you. It's always been you."

Jillian knew what he meant. She also knew he was wrong. It wasn't her. It wasn't him, either. It was them.

She held his quiet gaze. Did he understand that?

As if by spoken agreement, when his lips touched hers, they let their eyes drift shut. And Jillian knew that, for her, it was a last-ditch effort to retain a secret, private place inside herself.

Just as she knew that there was no such place left.

The kiss was short, but no less intimate or powerful than the ones they'd shared just before it.

Reese broke away first and stepped back, his weight shifting unevenly on his wounded leg. "You ready?"

"Yeah." She cast a swift glance at Cleo. Then took a double take. "Reese! She moved." She pointed to where Cleo was now hovering. "She was in the water, near the edge, before . . . before . . ." She faltered, but when she looked back at Reese, she found herself smiling instead of blushing. "A few minutes ago." A lifetime ago. "And now she's moved several feet. I wish I'd seen it."

A knowing look crossed Reese's face, and she silently admitted she wouldn't have traded what had transpired between them over the last several minutes for anything, not even for Cleo.

"If you think she'll be okay, why don't we go check out your clinic. It seems okay from here, but we should take a look."

"You're right. I'm going to need to get a handle on what my resources are. But this back area around the pond doesn't look so bad. Maybe I'll finally have some luck and Cleo won't need my help." She didn't let herself think about the nestlings. There was nothing she could do for them at this point except wait.

She turned and took a step back toward the renovated outbuilding that now served as her treatment center located at the other side of the rear area of the compound. Reese took her hand and fell into step beside her.

She liked the feel of his fingers twined with hers. And it seemed the most natural thing in the world to shorten her stride to accommodate his limp.

NINE

Several hours had passed by the time she and Reese had finished a rough categorization of the damage. It hadn't been easy for her. Several times, usually when she thought she was handling it pretty well, she'd find something, a broken chunk of equipment or a twisted piece of furniture, and the overwhelming realization of the depth of her predicament would threaten to consume her. And every time Reese was there. Sometimes with just a steady look, sometimes with a touch, and more than once with a quick, tight hug.

She might have been able to handle all of this without him, but she didn't want to contemplate how much worse it would have been. And she didn't beat herself up over taking what solace he offered her. He would be gone soon enough, and she would have plenty of time to shoulder the burden alone.

In the meantime, she'd absorb as much of his strength as he was willing to give, store it up for later. For all of the times he wouldn't be there, for all the times when she just wished he was.

"I think this is the last of it," Reese said as he entered the main treatment room they'd turned into a sort of inventory center. He had a small box under one arm and a large green trash bag in the other hand.

Her clinic had been relatively untouched, only a few shingles gone from the roof and the antenna for her two-way radio had been swept away. The chain-link pens and a good portion of the fence surrounding the property had been twisted or destroyed, but replacing them was the least of her concerns.

They'd spent the last thirty minutes transporting everything they'd stashed in the converted closet in the house to the clinic.

"We should probably try and move the mattress out here."

Jillian hadn't missed the strain on his face, nor had she missed how much more pronounced his limp had become. He'd taken something for the pain and even let her check the stitches. There was some redness, but it actually looked okay. His endurance and healing capabilities should have amazed her, but somehow, with Reese, only the opposite would have been a surprise.

But there was a limit, even for Reese Braedon.

"I think we've done enough. There is a cot in the back room," she added casually.

"You stay out here some nights?"

She nodded. "There are times I need to attend to some animals so regularly, it just makes sense to stay close by."

He hefted the bag onto the long counter and folded his arms on top of it. "You give so much of yourself to your work. Do you leave any for yourself? For your family?"

"My work is for myself," was all she would say, could say. "I can catalog the rest of this stuff. Why don't you go in the back and take some weight off of that leg for a while?"

Reese turned and grabbed a stool. He pulled it over, hoisted himself up, and propped his leg on the counter next to the bag. "Satisfied, Doc?"

More than she wanted to admit. She wanted his company, wanted him nearby, where she could look up and see him whenever she wanted to.

"You know, I never asked, but it must be tough financing an operation like this," Reese said. "How do you do it?"

What she didn't want to do was discuss her family. And he'd unknowingly asked her to do just that.

"I manage," she said, hoping he'd let her evade the issue.

"Grants? Private funding?"

She released a small sigh. She should have known there'd be a price to pay for getting to keep him near. There was always a price when she got something she wanted.

"My partner, Cole Sinclair," he went on, "got married a while back. His wife runs a school for disabled kids down in the Keys."

"That sounds wonderful. She must be a special person."

Reese's rusty smile surfaced again, making Jillian wonder just how special this woman was to him. It was disconcerting to realize how badly she wanted to know the answer to that.

"The night I met her I didn't think so. I thought she was using Cole, putting him in a situation he shouldn't have been put in, just to get her dolphin back."

"Whoa, I thought you said she ran a school for kids."

"She does. She uses dolphins to help reach kids who haven't responded to other forms of conventional treatment."

"I think I've read about that. About them helping autistic kids or something."

He nodded. "I wouldn't have believed it myself, except I've seen it. It's amazing."

"I take it your opinion of her has changed?"

He glanced away for a moment. He actually looked a bit . . . abashed. As if he'd only just now realized it had.

"Yeah, I guess so. Kira has turned Cole's whole life around. Before he met her . . . well, he was pretty messed up."

"And now?" she prodded gently, liking this uncertain side of Reese more than she dared to. There was a wistful quality to his voice she'd never thought to hear.

His smile surfaced again. "And now they make me sick. I think they only argue so they can . . . you know."

His smile faded. Hers grew. He was downright adorable like this. "Do what we were doing over by the pond a couple of hours ago?"

She had no idea where she got the nerve to say that. Reese's reaction was more than worth the risk. He looked like she'd just punched him in the gut.

There was a short pause, then he said, "The reason I brought her up was because she's a pro at fund-raising. I know she'd be willing to help you, at least give you some ideas."

He'd recovered his composure so quickly, Jillian wondered if she'd imagined his dazed expression. But she hadn't. What had gone through his mind?

Then his last sentence sunk in and her attention was caught up in figuring out how to answer him without telling him anything she didn't want him to know.

Reese saw her close him out as effectively as the steel hurricane shields had shut out Ivan.

Why was she freezing him out now? What had he said?

"I appreciate the offer," she said, her tone remarkably even, considering the change in her expression.

"But you're not going to take me up on it, are you." It was not a question.

"I'll think about it. I have a lot on my mind."

"Don't call us, we'll call you," Reese shot back, his sudden irritation rising quickly to the surface.

"Are you always so testy when someone doesn't jump at your gracious offers of help?"

"Are you just giving up, then?" he demanded. His arm swung wide as he gestured to the surroundings. "It's not a no-hoper, you know. You *can* fix this."

"I plan to."

That seemed to set him back, but only for a second.

"It's not going to be cheap, Jillian." He leaned forward. "Why won't you let me help? You've got this complex about having to do everything yourself. This is one battle you don't have to fight alone."

"And what do you know of my battles, Reese?" Even as she asked she knew it was a dumb question. The answer was in his eyes, had been there every time she'd looked at him. This was a man who knew more about battles and pain and being alone than she'd learn in two lifetimes. He knew.

And how she wished she hadn't asked.

"I know you've been hurt. But you're a battler, you're no stranger to a bit of hard work." His temper thickened his accent. "But we all need help, mite."

"What about you?" she asked, wanting desperately not to be the one on the defensive. "You don't strike me as the kind of man who sits around and lets others do for him. You won't even take care of a simple thigh wound." Her pulse rose along with her temper. "You took your job as an evac assistant like you were on a personal crusade. You stormed onto my property and actually tried to carry me out of here. So don't go telling me—"

She broke off when the stool he'd been sitting on crashed to the tiled floor. In the next second her arms were imprisoned in his big hands, and he bent his face down close to hers.

"You don't know why I came here, Jillian. But you were right about one thing, it *was* a job. And I take my jobs seriously, just like you—otherwise, why bother? Right?" He shook her lightly, his grasp tightening. He closed the gap between them until barely a whisper separated his mouth from hers.

"But even I know when I need help, Jillian." He took a deep breath, obviously trying hard to calm things back down. "I've got money," he said, his tone lower, but just as intense. "I've got contacts, I'm willing to help you. So why don't you stop blowing me off and tell me why you're really refusing to let me help here?"

"Fine!" she exploded, shoving hard against his chest. He didn't budge, but her temper had already pushed her past the point of caution. "I've learned the hard way that when you ask for help from people, the payback is always more than you can afford. So I stopped asking."

"You also stopped giving. Except to your animals."

"You got that right, buster. And they appreciate it, which is more than I can say for just about everyone else I've ever tried to—"

"To what, Jillian?" he broke in ruthlessly. "To love? To care for? Like who, Jillian?" His voice dropped to a dark, rough whisper. "Who took your love and threw it back at you?"

She felt her face drain of all color and warmth. Her mouth opened, then shut. He did know.

"Tell me!"

"Why?" she shouted, suddenly back in the thick of it, as if he hadn't just pulled the rug out from under her neatly organized little life. "So you can hurt me too? Well you can't, Reese Braedon, because I won't let you. You hear me?" She thumped his chest. "I won't let you." And to her eternal shame her last word erupted on a choked sob.

In the next instant she was engulfed in his embrace. He held her head tightly against his chest, his cheek resting on the top of her head as he ran his other hand up and down her back.

"I'm sorry, Jillian. It was none of my damn business." He pressed a kiss against her head, then leaned down and pressed another one on her temple. "I know what it's like to have it tossed back in your face," he whispered roughly. He tilted her face up so she had to look at him. "And I'm a bastard for badgering you at a time like this." He dropped a soft kiss on her lips, then let his forehead rest on hers.

"It's just . . ." He reached a rough fingertip up to trace away the wetness that had brimmed over her lower eyelid, but hadn't enough steam to form a tear. "I like my life clean. Neat. No clutter. I get work, I do the best job I can, I get paid for it, I go on to the next job. Simple. And I've made damn sure it stayed that way. But now . . . with you . . ."

He broke their gaze and looked down for a moment, then finally met her eyes again. "I want to help you, Jillian. No strings, no payback. Nothing. I just want to help."

Jillian trembled with the effort of keeping her cheeks dry from the flood of tears pleading for release. He would break her heart. Damn him. He wouldn't even try, or mean to. But he would. Because she'd let him.

Even now, when she was still thinking clearly enough to tell him no, to make it clear his help was the last thing she wanted, she knew it would take very little, shamefully little, to get her to say yes. Say yes to just about anything he wanted to give her.

Only the one thing she suspected she was coming to want more than anything she'd ever allowed herself to yearn for, was the very last thing he'd give her.

His heart.

Damn him.

She sniffed. Not as indelicately as she'd have liked to. And another crack fissured across her heart when he smiled.

"I have money, Reese," she said, her voice still clogged with unshed tears.

"Enough to repair this place?"

"Enough to rebuild it entirely if I wanted to."

Reese shifted back, then broke away to lift himself up to sit on the counter. Before Jillian could begin to think, Reese tugged her between his legs and looped his arms around her shoulders. He wasn't about to let her put any distance between them. She knew it was a lost cause right then. Because she didn't mind a bit.

"Can I ask where? How?"

"Family money."

"So you're loaded, huh?"

She knew he was teasing her, suffered the painful irony of realizing she'd finally found a man who wouldn't be swayed by the almighty dollar. But she'd spent too many years protecting herself to let all her barriers go at once.

"It's all in a trust fund. I can use it only for the rehab clinic." The story she'd told dozens of times, very convincingly and without a whit of guilty conscience, sounded hollow to her ears and exactly like the bald-faced lie it was.

The room was silent for several seconds. Jillian knew better than to look up at Reese. She kept her gaze at shirt-pocket level.

"So," he said calmly, as if there had been no break. "Why haven't you expanded?"

For a moment she thought she'd gotten away with it.

"Or doesn't your trustee let you make big, intelligent decisions like that?"

He knew. She looked up at him. "I don't want to expand. My operation here is fine." She shrugged. "Besides, the area really doesn't demand a larger facility and—"

"And you know that if you grow any larger you'll have to hire real personnel, maybe even take on a partner. And you'd rather stop altogether than have to do that."

Bull's-eye. Smack in the center of her heart.

But some part of her realized he'd been too damn certain of his statement for it to be all guesswork. And he didn't know her all that well. At least not about her background.

"Is that why you quit, Reese?" she asked harshly. Going on the defensive was becoming a habit around him. "Why you went private? So you could be in control of who you worked with? Who you didn't work with? So you could control who you'd be forced to get close to in order to do your job effectively without risking any . . . what was it you called it? Clutter?"

She'd scored a direct hit herself, if his instantly closed expression was any gauge.

But she found she didn't like hurting him any more than she liked being hurt. Her temper quelled. "Doesn't feel so great, does it?" she asked softly.

He blew out a long breath and pulled her against him. "What a pair of no-hopers we make, huh?"

She went easily, letting her arms slide around his waist as she rested her cheek against his chest. If her time with him was measured, she'd rather listen to his heartbeat than his angry words.

"It *was* a trust fund," she said at length. "My father left it for me. It drove Regina—my mother—crazy that he'd left me in control of it."

"Why? Didn't he leave her any?"

"No. But it wasn't as heartless as it sounds. My parents divorced when I was five. By the time my father died, Reggie had latched on to husband number two. And she'd made damn sure his bank account was up to her new standards."

"New standards?"

A familiar tension tightened across Jillian's forehead. This was the conversation she'd wanted to avoid. "Let's just say that after she divorced my dad, Reggie decided to take the safe path, the secure path. For my mother, security is money. And she found that the most efficient way to achieve that goal was to marry it. Which she has. Several times."

"Did she love your dad?"

The question took her off guard. She answered without thinking whether or not she should. "You know, I used to spend agonizing hours wondering about that. I wasn't sure when I was younger, but when I was in college, I . . . had this relationship." She snorted in disgust.

"Blinded by romance and foolish love, I was certain then that my mother had loved my father more than anything. So much that she'd shunned the whole concept of love when the marriage failed. It was so tragic, so romantic. I was so stupid, thinking I had it all figured out, that when I explained to her that it was okay because Thomas really loved me, she'd understand my decision to marry a man whose aspirations began and ended with being a science professor. Or so I thought."

"I take it she didn't."

"The only thing Regina understands is money and the security it brings. And she's convinced that anyone can be bought. Love doesn't enter into it. Fortunately for her, she's a beautiful, cultured hostess any man would be proud to claim as his own. His job is simply to provide the money. In stocks, bonds, property, whatever. And in her name. It's all upfront and very civilized."

"And you think this is mercenary, horrible."

Jillian tilted her head back. "It doesn't matter what I think. It's her life. She won't change."

"But she thinks you should, right? That's why she hates to see you spend money on your clinic when you should be in West Palm, getting your hair and nails done to snag that millionaire."

Jillian knew she looked stunned. She recovered quickly, though. "I don't need to marry anyone for money or anything else."

"No?" he asked gently, lifting her chin with his finger.

"No."

"You never married your college sweetheart?"

She pulled her chin away and looked down, wishing she had the strength to keep looking him in the eye. "No."

"And you're happy here, alone."

Her head came up, temper flaring again. "You should understand that one, Reese. No clutter. And yes, Regina wanted me to marry rich, preached for years that it was my best chance at controlling my own destiny. Marrying for love was foolish and unnecessary in her eyes. In fact, she made damn sure I had every opportunity to see things her way." Thomas hadn't even bargained for a higher price. He'd taken the first figure Regina named—a fact she'd made certain to share with her daughter.

Jillian drew in a deep breath and squared her shoulders. "But I made my own destiny without falling into her trap. When I turned twenty-five, I got control of my trust fund, invested wisely, and now I answer to no one. No one!"

Reese gripped her shoulders, and it was only then she realized how badly she was trembling. How did he get her like this? And she knew deep down it wasn't the life-shattering events of the last twenty-four hours, that no matter when or where or how they might have met, he'd have brought her to this point anyway. Why him? Why now?

"You know what I think?" He jiggled her shoulders to get her full attention. "I think you were right. I think your mother was so wildly in love with your father that when he rejected her it destroyed something inside her, something fundamental to her ability to love again, to trust it could be returned, to even believe in it."

"And how in the hell did you come up with that analysis? Or are you talking from personal experience? Your own past?"

His jaw clenched tightly, but he didn't react to her challenge. "I have a confession to make."

"What?"

He nodded to the large green trash bag he'd carried over to the clinic. "When I went through your stuff, to pack for you, I found a photo in your drawer. Since you didn't have it out, I wasn't sure whether it was something you'd want to save—"

Jillian knew exactly what photo he was referring to. Her heart clenched, and her knees shook. She knew every individual grain of that black-and-white photo. She'd had a long love-hate relationship with it, had wanted many times to destroy it, but always stopped herself in time. Her breath caught in her throat as it occurred to her that since she'd kept it tucked in her bedroom dresser, the photo was likely somewhere over the Gulf of Mexico by now.

"Oh dear God," she whispered.

"It's in the bag, Jillian. I put it in there, just in case."

"But that bag split open when I fell—"

"I wrapped it in one of your sweatshirts. I checked it when I picked up your things. It was okay."

Instinct drove her into his arms, and she hugged him as tightly as she could. "Thank you. It's the only picture I have of . . . of the three of us." She pulled back, feeling suddenly too vulnerable. "My father hated having his picture taken. As you could probably tell from looking at it."

Reese was silent for so long, she finally looked up at him. He was staring at her, his expression unreadable.

"You know what I saw in that photo, Jillian."

She didn't want to go on with this, didn't want to hear him say it out loud, to confirm what she knew, had always known. And yet she heard herself asking him, "What? What did you see?"

His gaze intensified, locked on her, focused on her, connecting them in a way that was more powerful than any physical bond.

"I saw a woman very much in love with her husband."

The conviction in his voice shook Jillian. She'd never thought of him as a man who put much stock in emotions like love. Caring, helping, yes. But not something as vulnerable, as threatening as love.

It shook her worse to realize that she'd just defined her own feelings about love.

"I also saw a man whose mind was occupied with things other than his wife and child." His voice grew harsher. "Greater things, stupid things, wasteful things . . . I don't know. Just not what his wife wanted him to have on his mind when he was with her. She wanted him to be thinking of her. To look at her the way she was looking at him. And I don't think he did. Ever."

Tears burned in her eyes, but refused to fall. The photo was etched in her mind in perfect clarity. Her mind's eye kept focusing on the child that had been her. Had Reese noticed her? Or had his attention been captured by Regina's beauty and tragic longing?

Some inner force compelled her to ask. "What did you see when you looked at . . . the child?"

His body jerked slightly as if she'd hit him, then he stilled, tensed. For a second she thought he would set her away from him, but then he bent closer to her.

"I saw me, Jillian. I saw me."

Jillian's throat knotted, tears spilled over and ran down her cheeks unheeded. He knew. Reese had known what she'd felt when she looked up at her mother so long ago. What he'd just forced her to admit she still wanted today. To be loved. Simply. Totally. Just for herself.

Through her tears she stared into Reese's hard eyes and saw that same pain, that same yearning.

Dear Lord, not him too. Such a fine man. Who must once have been a fine boy; a sweet, trusting child.

There was no relief in the sharing. Her own hurt escalated in the knowledge that he'd suffered, too, that she hadn't been alone.

"Oh, Reese," she whispered hoarsely. She reached for his face and pulled it down to hers. And she kissed him, letting down every barrier she'd ever erected. Everything she felt, everything he'd made her feel was in her kiss.

In the next instant she was pulled hard against his chest, his mouth fierce and full against hers as she felt his walls tumble down on top of hers.

"Jillian," he whispered raggedly against her lips, his voice filled with undisguised yearning, heavy with newly acknowledged need.

"I know, Reese. I know." And then the time for talk was over.

Their kisses were dark and powerful. Reese took her mouth, demanded possession of it at the same time he awarded her possession of his.

Her hands left his cheeks and trailed down to his chest. It was rock, living rock; hot and pulsing under her searching fingertips. She clutched at his shirt, pulling upward, needing, wanting, to have her hands on his bare skin.

Reese yanked it over his head and claimed her mouth again. She let him. Tasted his desire for her as her hands felt it.

His chest was sleek, hard, his skin molded

tightly around every muscle. Her fingers charted it all, the sensations moving through them into her body. Her skin heated, her muscles grew languorous, and the most poignant ache tightened slowly between her legs.

"Reese," she whispered. It was part worshipful, part pleading.

He bent lower, his mouth finding the side of her neck. "Sweet Jillian," he breathed in her ear.

Jillian opened her eyes, only then realizing they'd drifted shut. His chest filled her vision and she leaned into it, her mouth exploring the course her fingers had taken. Reese clutched her head in his hands but didn't stop her as he leaned back against the wall, drawing her with him.

She tasted the fine, crisp hairs that bisected his pectorals, then dropped small kisses on the swell of the muscle leading to his nipple. It was rigid, distended and begged to be tasted. She did. Reese bucked beneath her, a deep groan vibrating the skin beneath her cheek.

She withdrew her tongue.

"No," he rasped. "Feels . . . wonderful."

She smiled against his chest, reveling in her newfound power to distract, to disarm. The idea that she was able to pleasure this man was heady stuff indeed. She let her tongue blaze a provocative trail across his chest to his other nipple, where she feasted again. She felt his hips rise against her stomach again and again, establishing a sinuous rhythm that seduced the muscles between her legs into relaxing and contracting in a similar primal beat.

She was on fire, she was melting, she was exploding. She thought she might die before she figured out how to find that elusive thing which would satisfy this hunger, this craving, this need that pushed her, drove her, controlled her.

Suddenly Reese's hands were on her, tugging at her shirt. She felt the humid Florida air move across her skin, electrifying it. The feel of the cotton dragging across her breasts was wildly erotic, and she wanted it to go on and on. Then when the shirt was gone, she knew she wanted more. She wanted Reese on her. His hands, his mouth, his tongue.

So demanding was the ache, she cupped her own breasts, seeking to ease the pain any way she could, as fast as she could.

Reese groaned, and her gaze flew up to meet his. Her hands stilled, but when she began to move them, he stopped her.

"Don't. I have never seen . . . anything so . . . beautiful." His voice was barely more than a gravelly rasp. His chest heaved as he devoured her with his electric blue gaze.

Jillian had a sudden flash of insecurity. Her hands were small, yet they almost completely covered her breasts. A lifelong sense of inadequacy reared its threatening head, and she pleaded with him silently to help her past this barrier.

"Drop your hands now, mite. Let me look at you."

She did. His eyes burned brighter, hotter. She hadn't thought it possible. Just as she hadn't thought the ache below her belly could grow more intense. She was wrong, deliciously wrong, on both counts.

"Perfect pearls. That's what they are, Jillian."

Her shoulders squared, her spine straightened, until what little flesh she possessed was pushed proudly toward him.

In a dazed, erotic haze she saw Reese's hands move lower. Her breathing became shallower as she awaited his touch.

But his hands stopped at the snap to his jeans. She was riveted, her complete attention caught as he freed the shiny button.

There was no mistaking that he was aroused. He was a big man, and apparently there was no exception to any part of him.

"Can you see how you excite me, Jillian? Can you?" He lowered the zipper slowly, the teeth straining to hold together the taut denim covering his arousal.

She nodded, feeling her throat go dry at the same time as her palms began to sweat. She wanted to touch him, to hold him. To feel that desire pulse in her hands, in vibrant, life-giving proof that his need was as strong and mighty as hers.

Then he was bared for her to see. And he was glorious.

TEN

Jillian lifted her hands, then clenched them into fists at the last moment. She felt a sudden intense rush of intimidation.

He leaned back against the wall, but the bright fire in his eyes belied his casual pose. "Take it, Jillian. Hold it. It's like this because of you."

Her hands uncurled, and she reached for him. Hot, satiny, rigid, the skin so soft, yet it covered a hardness she'd never felt. He jerked in her hand. The muscles between her legs clenched in response.

The counter he sat on was waist-high to her. All she had to do was bend her head, just slightly.

"Yes. Go ahead. Please."

He tasted musky, sweet. And the mere knowledge that a part of him had entered her body—even her mouth—captivated her so fully, she could think of nothing else, was reduced to instinct and need.

She tightened her lips and let her tongue stroke him. He surged against her, filling her until she couldn't take any more. Never in her life had she felt this primal, never had her life been brought to such a simple common denominator. She wanted one thing. Above all else, including her next breath.

And it wasn't having him in her mouth.

She slid her mouth slowly off of him and felt his shaking groan in every nook and cranny of her soul. It echoed deep inside her, matching her own.

She lifted her head, knowing what she wanted, yet suddenly at a loss as how to get it. Her knees were locked against the trembling need that threatened to drive her to the floor. Her breasts ached . . . She needed, she needed . . .

Her hands found him again as she stepped closer between his legs, until the edge of the counter pressed into the soft skin of her belly. Her breasts needed him, to feel his touch. She heard him gasp as she bent forward.

When she brushed the tip of him across first one breast, then the other, they both moaned in unison.

Slowly, her gaze traveled up across the ripples of muscle lining his abdomen, across the swell of his chest, to the rigid vein standing in stark, pulsating relief against the side of his neck, to his jaw, clenched, his beautiful mouth compressed, then finally to his eyes.

And there she found everything she'd ever wanted.

Her mouth opened, though she had no idea what she was going to say. She didn't have to say anything.

"Take off your pants." The command was rough, uncivilized. And exactly what she wanted to hear.

Without looking away, she complied. His jeans hit the floor just as hers did.

The instant she was bare to him his hands uncurled from their white-knuckled grip on the counter's edge. He leaned forward and clasped them around her hips.

He lifted her easily, until her knees straddled him. She tried to keep from knocking against his bad leg, but his thighs were thickly muscled and . . . Any thought of his wound flew from her mind when she realized what he was about to do.

She looked down between them, saw his rigid length straining toward her hips . . . hips that suddenly looked so narrow . . . too narrow.

Her hands flew to his shoulders. She sunk her fingers into the dense muscle. "Reese!"

"Shhh. It'll be okay."

She locked her arms, leaning back from him as she sought reassurance in his face. "Have you ever . . . done this . . . with someone . . . like me?"

He let his actions speak for him as he settled her on top of him. She felt him breach her, sinking her deliberately, easily, over the tip of him.

He answered her slowly, his gaze solidly on her as he slid her down onto him. "I have *never* . . .

done *anything* like this . . . with *anyone* . . . like you."

And then he was completely inside of her, so deep within her, filling her until she knew there wasn't a cell in her body that didn't feel him. And it was wondrous, magnificent.

"Relax, mite." He leaned forward to nuzzle her neck, not moving inside her.

She knew the cost, felt it in the steel under her fingertips, the rocklike length of his thighs between her knees as he strained to keep his hips from thrusting.

His breath was hot, the words he whispered in her ear, hotter. "Relax your knees." His hands continued to hold her hips until he felt her muscles loosen. Only then did they drift upward to cover her breasts.

She gasped and rocked forward. The motion thrust her hips down onto him, and a moan tore from her throat.

Reese bucked up in automatic response, but he stilled almost immediately. His hands remained on her breasts. "Sorry. Did I hurt you?"

"No," she answered, as surprised as she was truthful. She focused her thoughts on relaxing like he'd asked, feeling him slide a bit farther into her. Her breath sucked in little gasps as he lifted his hips ever so slightly beneath her. Her nails dug into his shoulders, but she didn't tense.

His head dropped forward, and his mouth closed over one nipple. She moved on him. He groaned and thrust under her again, but kept his mouth on her. He spread hot wet kisses across her chest much like she had his, capturing her other nipple. This time she started rocking on him, and couldn't stop.

The tightly coiled need inside her started to slowly unwind. She'd found what she'd hunted for earlier. The answer to her elusive need. Her body took over, going after it with a single-minded intensity that sent any thought but completion spiraling away.

Reese's hands dropped back to her hips to hold her, to control the rhythm. He slowed her, and she fought against it.

"Jillian, I don't want to hurt you."

"Dammit, Reese, you're killing me. Let go."

She tightened her knees, seeking to tighten the muscles inside of her. And then she found control over them. She clenched, he groaned. She moved, he followed. Her movements became wild, frenzied. She exulted in the sleek, powerful body under her that matched her thrust for thrust.

Gloriously, shamelessly, she rode him.

And he gave her the ride of her life.

And then she was there. On the brink of discovery, of capturing that mysterious something she'd . . .

Reese's hand found her, she leaned into it. And exploded. A scream of release was wrenched from her throat as her whole world rose up in a sudden swirling vortex of sensation, and then suddenly everything burst as if tiny firecrackers had been attached to each and every nerve ending in her body and they'd all gone off at the same time.

And in the center of the fiery explosion, Reese shouted her name and arched under her, finding his own release.

Jillian collapsed against him, her chest heaving, skin damp, pulse pounding so loudly, she couldn't think. Didn't want to think. She hadn't gotten over feeling yet. Thinking was a concept she simply couldn't realize.

Reese lifted his hand to her head, smoothing the tangled strands of her short hair with fingers still trembling from what had just taken place between them.

When he could, he cupped the back of her head and lowered his mouth to hers. He'd meant to kiss her gently then hold her against his chest again. But he found he couldn't leave her mouth. It was sweet and swollen, and he kept his lips gently on hers as their breathing slowed and their hearts gradually found their natural rhythms.

Languor crept over him, filling his muscles with sweet lassitude. And still his mouth stayed on hers. He wanted her right here like this, forever.

And then it hit him with the force as violent as the hurricane that had ripped apart her house.

For the first time in his life, he'd had unprotected sex. Reese Braedon, the man who controlled every aspect of his life within his power *never* left something as easy and important as . . . that . . . up to fate.

And he knew damn well she wasn't using anything.

He closed his eyes and let his mouth drift from hers down to nuzzle her neck. That's when the second blow struck.

Why in the hell was he still kissing her? Why wasn't he panicking? Why wasn't his mind instantly formulating all the ways to deal with this unplanned event.

His mouth landed on her pulse. And the sweet pressure of her life beating against his lips brought him the answer.

He wasn't upset because . . . he wasn't upset.

Holy bloody hell.

After a moment, Jillian shifted away from him. She pressed her cheek against his shoulder, then leaned forward to drop a light kiss beside his ear. "Reese, this . . . I feel . . . we need . . ." She tried to pull away from him.

His arms quickly circled her, holding her tightly to him. He turned his head so his mouth was against her ear. "No, don't. I know we'll have to talk about this. But not now, okay?"

She didn't squirm, but she didn't settle back in his arms either. "Reese—"

He sighed, not wanting it to get difficult yet. "Jillian, I imagine I'll screw this up quickly enough as it is. Just let me . . ." He pulled in another breath, held it, then let it slip slowly past his lips.

He dropped a kiss on her temple. "Just let me stay . . . inside you . . . like this . . . for a little while longer."

After what seemed like eons, he felt her relax. Joy, a fierce, unexpected sense of contentment filled him. He looked down at the top of her head and smiled. Never in his life would he imagine he'd be so damn lucky to be holding a woman like Jillian in his arms.

He didn't want to think about what was going to happen later. And there was always a later.

Suddenly Jillian tensed again in his embrace. His first thought was denial. To rebel against it being over too soon.

Then he heard it. The unmistakable sound that Jillian must have heard.

A helicopter. Close. And getting closer.

"Who in the hell would have a chopper here this soon?" Jillian asked, lifting her head from his chest.

Reese had a sick feeling he knew exactly who it was.

Reese managed to drag his pants on and locate his shirt fast enough to be only seconds behind Jillian. The instant she'd realized the helicopter was coming closer, she'd muttered, "Cleo," and was off of him and dressed in a flash, then out the clinic door.

Not exactly how he'd envisioned ending their interlude.

Reese paused in the doorway, watching Jillian motion the chopper toward the front corner of the compound diagonally across from the pond and Cleo. It was the only place with enough free space to land the machine.

It occurred to Reese as he limped across the littered grounds that instead of being disappointed about this sudden turn of events, he should be relieved. He was certain that Regina Ravensworth was in that helicopter, and equally certain that as soon as Jillian realized her mother had hired him, both of them would be politely invited to get the hell out of there.

He watched Jillian step back as she watched the helicopter swoop in. The wind created by the rotors whipped her short hair around her head and rippled her T-shirt against her small frame.

Yeah, relieved.

No sticky good-byes, no unwanted entanglements. No clutter. Just how he liked it. How Jillian liked it too. They should both be downright ecstatic.

So why was his heart pounding harder the closer he got to the slowly descending chopper? Why was there an ache tightening in the center of his chest that felt like it might strangle him? And why in the hell did he feel like nothing in his life had prepared him for what he was likely to endure in the next several minutes?

He stopped several feet behind Jillian. He wasn't even certain she knew he was there. Maybe that was just as well.

No one descended from the helicopter until the rotors had slowed to a pace that no longer kicked up any wind. Then the small hatch door opened.

Jillian took a step forward as the door inched open, but froze in midstride as the slender brunette stepped out and graciously allowed the pilot who'd scrambled around the front of the chopper to help her down.

"Mother?"

"Jillian, darling!"

Reese watched as the older woman slid her silk scarf from her perfectly coiffed head and tucked it into her small shoulder bag. She was wearing a khaki-colored silk ensemble with razor sharp pleats bisecting the pant legs and shoulders. No visible wrinkles marred the expensively tailored fit. With gold at her neck, ears, and wrists, and expensive imported leather sheathing her dainty feet, Reese imagined Regina Ravensworth, at fifty-something, still managed to turn heads young and old wherever she went.

Regina kept her gaze fixed on her daughter. Reese noted how careful she was not to look at the rest of the property. Her set expression told him that she intended to sweep her daughter out of here and never allow either of them to reflect on what he was certain would simply be referred to in the future as "that unfortunate incident."

Reese's pulse kicked into gear again—only this time in irritation, rather than trepidation. Didn't she have any idea how much this place meant to Jillian?

Regina rushed to her daughter, who hadn't budged since the chopper door had opened. "Jillian, sweetheart, I'm so relieved!"

Reese watched Regina stop just in front of her motionless, silent daughter. She hid it well, but Reese could tell she was uncertain how to proceed, uncertain whether or not Jillian would rebuff any further show of affection. He could only imagine how uncomfortable that made a woman like her feel. It didn't bother Reese at all to watch her deal with it.

After a split second, Regina let her hands drop to her sides and satisfied herself with a quick air kiss beside her daughter's cheek.

Jillian made no return gesture. It wasn't until Regina stepped back and looked her daughter up and down that Jillian finally moved. She shifted her weight from one foot to the other, finally folding her arms across her waist. "Regina. Why are you here?"

"Well, isn't that a bit obvious?" Perfectly sculpted nails fluttered as she spoke. "I was worried half to death when I heard you wouldn't evacuate."

Jillian's eyebrows narrowed. "And just how did you hear that?"

"I . . . have my sources." She hurried on.

"And when I didn't hear from Mr. Braedon here, you can imagine how frantic I became."

Jillian's arms loosened, her hands dropped to her hips. "You knew the name of the evac person sent here? Your sources must be incredible."

"Well, of course I knew who he was."

"Jillian," Reese spoke for the first time.

Jillian looked over her shoulder, clearly unsurprised at his presence behind her. "What?"

Regina didn't give him a chance to answer. She took a step toward Reese. "And if you think you'll be paid for this rescue effort, you are sorely mistaken. I understood you were considered the best—"

"Regina, he's a volunteer. He doesn't get paid for this." She glanced at Reese. "Do you?" She shrugged and went on before either Regina or Reese could speak. "It doesn't matter." She faced Regina. "It wasn't his fault I didn't leave. In fact, it's *my* fault his life was put at risk."

"Jillian—"

"Mr. Braedon," Regina said, interrupting his second attempt to explain. "I appreciate your tact regarding my instructions, but when I hired—"

"I won't take money for this, Mrs. Ravensworth," Reese cut in, his frustration growing at the way this conversation had spun quickly out of his control. "I know you think you had Jillian's best interests at heart, and I can't blame you for wanting to secure her safety."

Jillian turned slowly toward him. "Reese, what are you talking about?"

Reese sighed, but finished what he was saying to Regina, although he kept his gaze locked on Jillian while he spoke. "In your place, I can honestly say I'd have done the same thing. Or at least tried. But she's a grown woman"—Reese's body seconded that, his muscles clenching too tightly as he watched the horror of comprehension dawn slowly on her small face—"and while I don't agree with her reasons for staying here, risking her life, I do think she has the right to make that choice herself."

He turned his head to Regina for a split second. "So you don't have to fire me. I stopped working for you several hours ago."

"Reese?" Jillian took a half step in his direction, then stopped. Her hand lifted, then dropped to her side.

Reese closed the small gap, wanting to touch her, not knowing if he'd ever be given that right again. He certainly wasn't going to force the issue now, in front of her mother.

"Jillian," he said quietly, although he sensed Regina was hanging on his every word. "I should have told you. But Regina had asked me not to. And when I realized we were trapped here anyway, I didn't see the point in angering you with the information."

"Angering me?" Her eyes widened. "Angering me?"

"I didn't know what the deal was with you and

your mother, then. I don't know it all now. But no matter why I was here to rescue you, the fact is it was still my job and I failed. We were stuck together no matter what. Put yourself in my place. Would you have told me?"

Jillian's eyes remained hard for several nerve-racking moments, then her shoulders relaxed and her jawline softened. "I suppose not."

Her chin dipped, and Reese lifted it back up without thought as to how the action would be perceived by Regina, not really caring. "I'm sorry," he said so softly, only Jillian could hear. "I would have told you. Whatever happened between you and your mother, you have to know it has nothing to do with me. Once I realized we were trapped . . . Well, I was on my own. What I did, anything I did, I did because I wanted to."

"You're right about one thing. You were just hired to do a job." She lifted her chin from his touch and stepped back. "And now it's over."

She turned away.

"Jillian!" Regina stepped forward, her tone strident.

Jillian turned back around, resignation clear on her face. "You got what you wanted, Mother. I'm alive. I'm safe."

"But, but . . ." Regina sputtered, then quickly regained her control. "Jillian, dear, surely you can see now that you can't stay here." At her daughter's immediate defensive posture, she amended, "At least, not until you renovate . . . or whatever. I insist you come stay with Harold and me for a . . . while. This must have been a simply horrifying ordeal for you." She looked at Reese, speculation over the exact details of said ordeal clear in her expression. "I'm sure that after a few months . . . or weeks, you'll be in a much better frame of mind to deal with"—she waved her arm around, but didn't actually look—"all of this."

"I'm not going anywhere, Regina." Jillian raised her hand to deflect her mother's continued attempt to persuade her. "I have a lot to do and the sooner I begin, the sooner I can get this clinic operational again." She paused for a moment, searching for the right words to placate her mother. "I appreciate your offer. And your help." Jillian resisted the urge to look at Reese. "Really. But I'm okay."

And Reese was a huge part of why she was okay, but his part in all this was over, and the sooner she came to terms with that, the better.

The slight tightening of the skin around Regina's lips and the stiffening of her shoulders told Jillian just how upset her mother was with her rejection. But she refused to feel guilty.

She knew Regina had been concerned about her, in her own way. But Jillian was equally certain that Regina had seen Hurricane Ivan as the perfect means to convince her daughter that her current lifestyle was simply untenable, and had used it as a way to get her daughter back under her control.

Well, she'd failed. Again.

"Give Harold my best."

Jillian turned away but hadn't taken a step when her throat constricted and her chest tightened as visions of what had happened between her and Reese just prior to her mother's arrival flooded her mind.

She paused, unable to banish the images, to push Reese mentally aside as she had her mother.

Lord, but those incredible moments with him, when he'd been inside her, when he'd taken her to nirvana and back, had been the singularly most intense experience of her life. And as much as she should probably regret them, she couldn't.

And doubted that she ever would, no matter how miserable the ensuing days, weeks, and months ahead became without him.

It had happened. Magnificently, fiercely, naturally. But it wouldn't happen again.

She looked back at Regina. "If you have room, I'm sure Mr. Braedon would welcome a ride back to the mainland. I know he'll want to contact his partner and check on his property in the Keys."

Regina looked from her daughter to Reese, then slowly back again. "Jillian?"

The questions imbued in that simple one-word question were many, and Jillian wasn't able to pretend she didn't understand them. Might as well get past this too. It would save her from another visit or call from Regina where she'd be forced to rehash it anyway. Easier to do it now, before the pain was a raw festering thing and talking about it would be like picking at an open wound.

She faced her mother. "Yes?"

Regina stepped closer and dropped her voice to a whisper. A stage whisper. "Tell me you didn't do anything . . . foolish."

"Not that it's really any of your business, mother, but if you're asking if Mr. Braedon and I were . . . intimate, then the answer is yes."

Regina's hand flew to her throat. "Really, Jillian! Haven't you learned anything from your past with Thomas and that environmentalist . . . that Laxalt man, what was his name?"

"Richard."

"Yes, Richard. I mean, I know I've encouraged you to, you know . . . socialize. But as I've told you over and over, there are certain men who just aren't . . . appropriate."

"You mean men with less money than me? Men who see dollar signs when they look at me? Yes, Mother, I know all about those men. Reese isn't one of them."

Regina remained silent for several moments as she stared at her daughter. "It's not worth it, Jilly," she said quietly.

Jillian felt an immediate burning spring to the backs of her eyelids. Her mother hadn't called her that since . . . since she was a very small child. Before . . . before Regina lost her husband, lost everything.

"He'll break your heart." Regina reached out and took her daughter's hand. She squeezed it lightly. "Just remember one thing, the pain lasts far longer than the pleasure." She dropped her hand and stepped back, then turned.

"Mother."

Regina paused, then looked back over her shoulder. Jillian thought she saw a suspicious glimmer in her mother's eyes, but since Regina would die before she'd let her mascara run, she must have imagined it.

"I'm sorry," she said softly.

"For what?"

"I'm sorry Daddy hurt you so badly."

The glimmer became a wet glare across Regina's pewter-gray eyes. She managed a quick nod, then walked toward the chopper.

Jillian wiped the back of her hand across her eyes and watched as her mother spoke hurriedly to the pilot, then let him help her into the cockpit. She started to wave, but her mother was staring out the front windshield. She let her hand drop limply to her side. Suddenly she felt very drained. She turned around, and stumbled right into Reese.

He took her upper arms in a gentle grasp. "You okay?"

She nodded, but didn't look up at him. No one should have to deal with all of this in one day, she thought dejectedly. Now she had to contend with Reese.

And if her mother's good-bye had been difficult, she was certain the one with Reese would prove worse. For her at least.

Taking a deep breath, she squared her shoulders

and looked up at him, but before she could speak, the pilot rushed up to them.

"Uh, Mr. Braedon, Mrs. Ravensworth would be happy to fly you back to the mainland, but she'd appreciate it if you would come now, sir."

Jillian noticed Reese didn't even look at the man. His gaze was riveted on her.

"Jillian?"

His hold didn't tighten, his voice was rough, but no more than it was normally. Jillian searched his face for a clue as to how he felt. Was he asking her permission to stay? Would he if she asked? And for how long? She searched desperately for the words to tell him she didn't want him to go. No strings, no promises, no clutter.

But they didn't come. Instead she heard herself say, "Maybe you'd better go. I'm sure Regina will alert the authorities that I'm here." She tried not to see the doubt in Reese's eyes.

He wouldn't stay, and even if he did, it would only intensify the agony when he did go—which she knew he would. But she knew he'd make sure she was taken care of. He was that kind of man. It would have to be enough.

"I have enough supplies to last me. And I'll make sure your truck is safe. It's still there, isn't it?"

Reese only nodded, his expression still unreadable. After an interminably long time, he jerked his head up to face the pilot, and nodded his assent.

The pilot returned the acknowledgement and

headed back across the grass toward the waiting helicopter.

Not until then had Jillian felt the impact of what was going to happen. He was leaving her. She would likely never see him again. He could easily send someone for his truck and probably would. No clutter that way.

She stepped back, pulling her arms from his grasp. Better to make this as easy as possible. No tears or long, uncomfortable good-byes. After all, what did one say to a man she'd met only yesterday, but thirty minutes before had ridden like a wild wanton? It's been fun?

She started to tremble under his scrutiny as it became progressively darker. If he didn't leave quickly, it wasn't going to be a clean break. The tears were too close to the surface. *Oh God*, she prayed, *please let me at least end things this once without humiliating myself.*

And suddenly she was in his arms, and his mouth was hard on hers. He didn't kiss her, he took her. He claimed her lips, branded her with his taste, his textures, his touch. And at the exact moment she felt her knees begin to sway, he set her away from him.

"I know you want this to be over," Reese said roughly. "And you're probably right. But things aren't that simple."

Hope spurted, then died. Jillian realized he was referring to the fact that they hadn't used any protection earlier.

"I'll uh, let you know," she said quietly, knowing it would be easy enough to track him down. Wondering if she would. A baby . . . Reese's baby.

His mouth tightened, and she felt her heart stop. The blur of emotions stirring in his blue eyes was too potent for her to allow herself to see . . . to believe in. And yet part of her, the part that would leave with him, pounded hard in her chest. And she silently urged him to say it . . . tell her what he was thinking.

"I don't make promises I'm not sure I can keep. Not the ones you need, at any rate. But I do take responsibility for my actions. If you're pregnant, we'll deal with it together. That's a promise."

No. She started to shake her head. No! She didn't want to hear this. At that moment she despised honesty.

Then he reached out and traced a finger across her lower lip. She froze under his touch, knowing it was likely the last one she'd ever get from him.

It took everything she had not to moan in despair when his hand dropped away.

"What I can't promise you, Jillian, is that I won't be back anyway."

Through dry, hot eyes she watched him walk to the waiting helicopter.

ELEVEN

Reese entered the small suite of offices he shared with Cole Sinclair and slapped the folder he'd been carrying on his desk.

"Braedon?"

Reese sighed, then shrugged in a vain attempt to relieve some of the tension that seemed to be a permanent part of his shoulders and neck these days. Along with the bloody headache, bad attitude, and generally piss-poor outlook on life.

He ducked his head into Cole's doorway. "Yeah?"

"You get that thing with Mr. Tomlinson wrapped up, okay?"

Reese nodded. "Said he'd need us again next month when he has that fund-raiser up in West Palm."

"Sounds like you're making quite a name up there among the moneyed set. First Mrs. Ravensworth, now Frank Tomlinson. Not bad, pal, not bad."

Reese tried not to snarl something rude in return. It wasn't his partner's fault that the very last place Reese cared to work, or even think about, was West Palm Beach.

"Right-o, mate," he said flatly. "Anything new come up?"

Cole stared at him for a moment, then gestured for Reese to enter the room. "Have a seat."

Reese pushed off the doorframe and moved over to the chair. His thigh was mostly healed, he'd taken the stitches out several days ago. It didn't ache at all anymore. He didn't allow himself to think about why that depressed him.

He started to sit down in one of the two navy blue padded chairs facing the desk when Cole rose quickly and gestured him away.

"Watch out, Reese. Other chair."

Reese barely stopped himself in time. He levered upright and looked behind him.

"Holy—" He bit off the curse. "A man can't turn around these days without being attacked by three-legged alligators and carnivorous iguanas."

"What was that?"

"What's Elvis doing here?" The two-foot-long iguana looked up at Reese and blinked. "And what's he doing in the chair?"

His partner's tanned skin darkened a shade. Only his wife, Kira, could make Cole react like a schoolboy caught passing notes in study hall. Normally Reese wouldn't miss a chance to razz Cole, but he remained silent, feeling envious for the first time. It irritated the hell out of him.

"He's not feeling too well. Can't get him to eat."

Reese heard the telltale signs of chirping. He should have heard the crickets right off. Would have if his mind hadn't been wandering . . . again.

He looked at Cole. "Think maybe he finally figured out he's supposed to eat plants and not bait?"

Cole shrugged. "Can't get him to eat anything."

"What does Kira say?"

Cole picked up a pencil and stared at it as he drummed a steady beat on his desktop. "Kira would just as soon Elvis found somewhere else to eat all his meals—whatever they may be. You know how she feels about him."

"Yeah, the same way she does about you. Resigned to the horrible fate of spending the rest of her life with you."

A slow smile crossed Cole's dark features. "Yeah, poor thing."

Reese still wasn't used to seeing that spontaneous reaction change his partner's face. There was a time when Reese thought—no, knew—he'd probably never see Cole smile again. Then Cole had met Kira Douglass . . .

But instead of the sparkling gray eyes of his partner's wife, Reese saw stormy, battle-shy ones.

And he wondered—for the millionth time in the last ten days—how Jillian was doing, whether or not Cleo's eggs had hatched, how the renovations were going . . . and if she laid awake at night aching for him even half as much as he ached for her.

"You look like you need to hit something. What gives? You haven't been the same since you flew back here on Mrs. Ravensworth's private chopper. Something else happen during the hurricane you haven't told me about? Aside from not getting paid, I mean?"

Reese knew Cole's last remark was meant to lighten things up. Cole's trust was complete, as was Reese's. He hadn't given a reason for refusing payment, nor had Cole asked him for one. Just as Reese wouldn't have asked had the situation been reversed.

Reese stared at Cole for a long moment, then down at his fingers picking at the hole in the knee of his jeans. Without looking up, he said, "How long did you know Kira before . . . before you . . . ?"

Cole looked confused, then grinned broadly as he watched his partner stumble over his words.

Reese heaved a heavy sigh then came straight out with it.

"When did you realize you loved her? I mean,

when did you know that going on without her would be worse than—"

"Living with my own sorry company for the rest of my life?" Cole stopped smiling, but his expression remained open. "Looking back I think some part of me knew all along. Otherwise I never would have agreed to help her." He released a sigh of his own. "But it wasn't until she left me that I did some serious thinking."

"And?"

"And I decided that if I fought half as hard to keep her as I did trying to ignore how I felt about her, I stood a pretty damn good chance of being happier than I had any right to be."

Reese nodded, but remained silent.

After a few moments, Cole said, "This wouldn't have something to do with that mousy little professor type Regina Ravensworth sent you to rescue, now would it?" The longer Reese sat there and scowled, the broader Cole's smile became.

"Up yours, Sinclair," Reese growled. But eventually his set jaw relaxed into the closest he could come to a smile.

"Wow. She must be some lady, my friend."

"She's no mousy professor type."

Cole laughed. "I can well imagine. So, what are you going to do about her?"

Reese looked at Cole, then turned his head and looked at Elvis. "You got a carrying cage for this reptile?"

"Yeah, why?"

"I think I know just the person to take a look at him."

Cole rose from his desk and went to rummage in his closet. He came out with a fiberglass, vented carrying case.

Once he'd loaded up the iguana, he handed it to Reese. "Take good care of him. I've grown sort of . . . attached to him."

"Yeah, I know how you feel."

"You? Fond of Elvis?"

Reese took the cage and peered inside, then let it dangle next to his thigh. He looked up at Cole, assuming an air of casual arrogance. "Nah. No pansy reptiles for me. I got a nine-foot gator waiting for me."

Cole smiled. "Just as long as he doesn't eat iguanas."

"Actually, it's a sheila." Cole raised his eyebrow. Reese had the grace to look sort of sheepish. "With three legs, name's Cleopatra."

"And you think I'm sick?"

Reese did smile this time. He walked to the door, then turned back. "I, uh . . . I might be gone for a few—"

"Take whatever you need. I can handle it."

Reese nodded. "Thanks. I owe you one."

"Nah. Way I figure it, we're just now getting even."

As Reese headed down the short hallway, Cole shouted, "And it's about damn time! Bring her back with you, Braedon. Kira and I want to meet her."

There was a brief pause. "And I'm not talking about the gator!"

Reese's smile lasted until he let himself out into the bright Florida sunshine.

"I'm gonna try, mate. Like I've never tried before."

Reese wasn't surprised to see that things hadn't improved much in the ten days since he'd left Caracoles Key. He knew that Ivan had only brushed the coast before heading back out into the gulf toward Texas and that most of the damage was south of the Sanibel area. But Jillian had been lucky. Some of the smaller spits of coastal land had been flattened.

Reese thanked the captain of the boat he'd hired to take him from Sanibel to Caracoles and headed toward Jillian's compound on foot. The first thing he noticed was that she'd moved his truck inside the now-warped fence, up closer to the house. Some of the smaller bits of wreckage had been moved into rubbish piles, but most of the work still lay ahead.

As he entered the grounds through a downed section of fence, he wondered if he'd be lucky enough to stay and help her with it. But luck had never been his claim to fame.

His grip tightened on the small carrying case. "Well, Elvis, let's go find her."

He was halfway to the house when he spied her

standing on the near side of the pond, a pair of binoculars perched on her nose.

His heart doubled, then tripled in time. He realized then how nervous he'd been. That a part of him had wondered if he'd imagined it all. The way she made him feel . . . like he'd finally found the one woman who could look at him and feel the same damn thing.

He was less than ten feet away when she whirled around, one hand flying to her chest as she let the binoculars bang against the front of her T-shirt.

"Reese." As quickly as she'd said his name, he watched her piece her control back together again. But that one unguarded moment was all he needed.

All he'd get. Unless he made damn sure he was around long enough to see that unguarded expression any damn time he wanted to.

Her expression was closed now, distanced. Reese vowed that, one way or another, that wouldn't last long.

"You here for your truck?"

"No."

Her gaze faltered for a split second, then held his firmly once more. "Oh. Then it must be the other loose end. You don't have to worry about that one. No clutter."

Something heavy and hot in Reese's heart shifted at her attempt to casually dismiss the life that might have begun as the result of what they'd shared ten days ago.

"I wasn't worried about that."

Her eyes widened slightly, then her shoulders squared and her chin lifted. Still a survivor.

Aw mite, he thought, *don't you know me better than that by now?*

"I wasn't worried, because I'm not sure I would have been upset if the outcome had been different."

Her mouth dropped open.

Good, now they were getting somewhere.

"What do you—?" Her attention was snagged by the case dangling from his hand. "What is that?"

Reese glanced down. "This is my excuse." He looked up and smiled at her. He wasn't certain of much, but he knew he wasn't going anywhere. Not now. Not yet. Not ever, if he had his way. And he bloody well planned to. "Pretty poor one too. His name's Elvis. He's an iguana. Belongs to my partner Cole."

"What's wrong with him?"

"Nothing now. He'd stopped eating, and Cole wasn't sure why. But on the way here I picked him up some crickets and he hasn't stopped eating since." He grinned at her confused expression. "Maybe he just needed to get out. He used to spend most of his time on the back of a Harley."

"Crickets? A Harley?"

"It's a long story." Reese's expression slowly sobered as Jillian looked from the carrying case to him.

"Why bring him to me?"

Lord what a loaded question. "Because there is no one else, Jillian," he answered, not even bothering to pretend he was still talking about the bloody iguana. "There never has been, and there never will be."

She stilled, staring at him, her expression . . . blank. Except for those eyes. Those ageless, survivor eyes. *Let me in. Believe in me*, he wanted to yell.

Jillian turned her back to him. He was amazed how much that hurt him. No, this wasn't going to be easy.

He stepped closer to her, wanting to touch her so badly, he ached with it. But he kept his free hand at his side.

She lifted her binoculars and aimed them across the pond.

After a short period of incredibly tense silence, Reese asked, "What are you looking for?"

"At. I'm watching Cleo's nestlings hatch."

"So they're okay?"

"I don't know if they'll all survive. Typically they don't, but there aren't any natural predators here, so their chances are dramatically improved. Still, a lot of water was dumped on that mound during the storm."

"But the chances are—"

"Shh." She waved her hand to silence him. "Listen."

Reese strained to hear something, anything.

"Do you hear that? Those tiny little gulping sounds?" Jillian turned to him, her eyes shining.

She imitated the sound for him. "Like that. Hear it?"

His pulse pounded, his blood ran hot. Nothing could have torn his gaze from hers, but he listened again. "I hear it."

"That's the nestlings. And if we can hear it from this distance, that means there's a bunch of them. Oh Reese, they made it! They made it!"

He almost pulled her into his arms right then and there, but at the last possible second, he managed not to. No. This had to be done right this time. In the right order. He wasn't going to give her any reason to run back to her little self-imposed shelter.

"Is there somewhere we can go?" he asked, his voice rough with the need he'd worked so hard to control. Her eyes darkened, and he almost lost it right there. "To talk?"

She nodded. Then after one last look across the pond, she slipped her binoculars from her head, jotted some notes in the notebook she'd been carrying, then stuffed it in the pocket of her baggy shorts. "I'm living in the clinic for the time being." She turned and headed in that direction.

Once inside, he lifted Elvis's travel case to one of the long shiny tables, then leaned back against it and watched her put away the notepad and binoculars.

When she was done, she stood against the sink across from him and loosely crossed her arms.

It was then Reese felt the panic. It clawed at

him, filling his stomach, then his throat. This was it. Where in the hell did he start?

"I came from a harsh country, Jillian," he said in a short burst. He drew a long, shaky breath, then let it out slowly. "I thought I was so damn tough. Didn't need anyone. Hell, I was only seventeen when I left to come here and I'd been on my own for almost three years."

"What . . . why?"

"You once said pearling was a tough, dirty business. Well, you were more right than you knew. My father had dreams. But they never seemed to work out. He worked hard, made a decent wage. But it wasn't what he'd planned. It wasn't enough. He started hitting the pubs. Eventually his hours on the job decreased, his wages went down, and he drank most of that.

"My mother . . . she tried every way she knew how to let him know it didn't matter to her. That she only wanted him. She'd have done anything to get his attention, to get him to understand. To the exclusion of just about everything else—me included. And when she realized the bottle held more allure than she did, she joined him inside of it. Things went to hell after that."

TWELVE

"How old were you?"

"I dunno. Twelve, thirteen. Old enough to know what was what and that I didn't have any."

"Oh, Reese."

The ache in her voice, the pain. He knew—*knew*—she understood. And the knowledge hurt him more than it soothed him. But he had to get it out.

"By the time I was fifteen, I didn't think anything or anyone was tougher than me. And all I wanted was to get out of there, as far away as I could go. It took me close to two months once I left Oz to reach America."

"But you were only a kid."

"I was a big kid. I spent most of what money I had on a passport and fake ID. That, a fast mouth, and a willingness to do just about anything can get you a job on a ship more easily than you'd think." He shook his head, an empty smile twisted his lips. "One day on the streets of Miami told me I didn't have even a passing fair acquaintance with tough. I was worse than a fish out of water, didn't fit in anywhere. The middle class blokes didn't half understand me, the ones who didn't think I was a wacko thought me a bloody savage.

"The Latinos didn't trust me, thought I was British and couldn't imagine I'd understand where they were coming from. I spent the next two years of my life just surviving."

"What happened?"

"I got busted for stealing food. The old man who owned the market didn't press charges. He gave me a job working for him instead." He focused sharply on her. "Jillian, for the first time in my life I was treated with respect."

"Somehow it doesn't sound like you were the type who fell all over the guy with gratitude."

"No. If I were Old Man Kotler, I'd have kicked my ass out in under a week. But he didn't. He busted my chops over every little thing. But he was always there. Even when I wished he'd go to hell, he was there. It wasn't easy, Jillian. But I tried. For the first time in my life, I really tried. When I decided I wanted to get my citizenship, he helped me."

"Where is he now? Still in Miami?"

Reese shook his head in a tight negative motion. "He was shot and killed right in front of me. I was twenty-one."

Jillian gasped, her hand flying to her mouth at the unexpected horror of his words.

"It was a robbery. Nothing you didn't hear every day on the news. I think they got about two hundred dollars." Reese looked at his feet. "I would have given my life for that old man." Reese felt the familiar hollowness inside yawn open as it always did when he thought of that day. So violent, so senseless.

"Reese." The word was an anguished whisper.

He looked up at her. "He always told me if I was going to be any kind of a man, that I should stand up for my beliefs. Well, I believed that an old man, or anyone else for that matter, should be able to go about the business of living without the fear of being gunned down. Not for two hundred bucks, not for two million." Reese heaved a deep sigh. "The short of it is that I knuckled down, begged, did anything I had to and went to work for Uncle Sam. Eventually DEA." He snorted. "Young hero cleans up Miami gutters."

"But you are a hero, Reese. Don't you understand? Mr. Kotler would be so proud of you."

"I know." He looked up at her again. "And I did the best damn job I could. I gave it everything I had to give. But eventually it wasn't enough for me. Or more to the point, I didn't have anything left to give. And when I knew I couldn't do my best, I got out."

"But you're still making a difference, Reese. You're still helping people."

"That's not what I'm trying to say." Without realizing it, he closed the small distance between them and took her by the shoulders. "The point is that I made a decision to do something, and I did it. I made it happen. I dedicated myself to it. Do you understand, Jillian?"

She nodded, her eyes guarded. "And I'm proud of you. But what does that have to do with me? You've also told me that you don't like messy ties, that you ruthlessly avoid anything that sounds like intimacy. That you want to be responsible only to the people who pay you for the service, and then, only until the job is done. Neat. Clean. No clutter." Her voice had risen steadily. She was shaking now. "So what in the hell has that got to do with me!"

He shook her, his face close to hers. "I can't let you go, dammit! There's this . . . hole . . . in me now. I think you are the only one who can fill it. I *know* you are."

"And what happens when you can't do that any longer, Reese? Huh? When you've given me all of yourself you can give? Do you walk away then too? I can't do that. I can't let you do that to me."

"So you'll stay here alone? Forever? There are no guarantees in life, Jillian. Or is it that you just don't want me?"

Her eyes widened. "Yes, I want you! Is that what you wanted to hear? Well, I said it. I want you, Reese Braedon. More than I've ever let myself want anything. And the instant I turned around and saw you behind me, I knew I'd take whatever you had to give me."

"And now?"

"And now I'm not convinced I'll be enough for you."

"What?" he barked in disbelief.

Jillian's fierceness crumpled, and she felt suddenly hollow and deflated. "You . . . you're intense, you know what you want, what you need. You go after it. You demand it and if it's not good enough, you leave and keep on going until you find something that is." She looked up at him. "I'd take part of you if I knew it was forever, but I don't think I can let you take all of me and know you'll walk away with it."

He lifted his hands from her shoulders and cupped her face, his hold on her unbearably gentle.

"And what if I told you I've stopped looking? That I've found it? I'm glad I left my old life, I like what I do now. But what I did was harder to handle than I realized. It was ugly and brutal and endless. If I'd stayed in it much longer, I doubt I'd have recognized the need I hadn't filled. That the emptiness I felt wasn't about job satisfaction. It was about me, about what I haven't let myself believe I could have. Until I met you. I looked into those wary gray eyes and saw myself, saw the other part of me." His expression gentled, his vulnerability plain for her to see. "What if I told you I've never been so sure of anything in my entire life?"

He was scaring her to death. He was big, and bold and strong and beautiful and fierce and she loved him. Loved him fiercely, boldly, strongly, completely. The way she'd always wanted to *be* loved.

And she was terrified to discover that the one thing she didn't do was trust him to love her like that in return. The pain was crushing. But it didn't alter the truth. She might love him like she'd never thought she'd love anyone. But she knew without a doubt that she wasn't strong enough to survive giving him her heart . . . only to have him change his mind somewhere down the road.

She wasn't even certain how well she was going to survive pushing him away now. But she had to. It was selfish, it was cruel, but it was survival. Hers.

That instinct had been too well honed, for too many years. And she found she couldn't give up its protection. Not even for Reese. Especially not for someone as dangerous to her as Reese.

"No," she whispered. Then more adamantly, with all her strength she said again, "No!"

She'd expected rage, defiance, a renewed assault or his immediate departure. So the utter pain that wracked his features, the brightness in his eyes, that faded swiftly into a bleak, cold place as if he'd just been cast back into that barren wasteland of his past struck her like a deathblow.

Her knees swayed. Pinpoints of light flickered in the periphery of her vision. Dear Lord, what had she done to him? What had she, in her selfish need to make sure she didn't suffer, done to the man she loved above all else?

Only that was apparently a lie. She didn't love him above all else. She'd put herself first.

Reese dropped his hands and took a step away from her. And it hit her then that this was it. There would be no more words, no more explanations, or entreaties. He'd literally opened himself up and laid himself bare for her—something she knew he'd never done for anyone else—and she'd tossed it back in his face. For what?

For what?

He was walking out of her life, and she knew she'd never see him, hear him, taste him, have him . . . Nothing. Not ever. For all eternity.

And she knew with a certainty so absolute, it rocked her violently. This was a mistake she'd regret every second, every hour, every month, every year . . . until the moment she drew her last breath.

He walked away.

What had she done?

"Reese."

To her eternal joy and shame, he stopped. And she knew it was already more than she deserved.

"I'm like you," she whispered hoarsely. "A survivor."

He didn't turn around. "I'm sure you'll bloody well survive this, too, then." His voice was rougher, deeper than she'd ever heard it.

"No. I won't."

He shifted his weight, then looked at her. "Well then," he whispered, his voice so depleted of emotion, it fairly vibrated with the absence of it. "I suppose that makes two of us."

Jillian took a tentative step toward him. "You really meant it, didn't you?"

"Of course I did. I've never lied to you." Frustration edged into his evenly spoken words, and she was amazed at his self-control.

Suddenly her throat closed and she felt panic claw at her as she realized how much she had riding on her next words. Only everything. Her whole life. Was this how he'd felt when he'd opened up to her moments ago? Did she have even half his courage?

"I meant what I said too." The words were forced out on a choked whisper. "About wanting you more than I've ever wanted anything."

"You have a damn funny way of showing it."

"I'm scared, Reese." That was so painful to admit.

"And you think I'm not?"

"I don't know. I know you have more courage than I could ever hope to have."

"You have courage, Jillian."

Her heart pounded painfully hard at the sound of her name on his lips.

"I'm selfish, Reese. I want it all, just for me. I thought Thomas loved me, and he left me for a nice fat check from my mother. And then there was Richard. I thought he understood, that he needed me. Then I found out he only needed the trust fund I was going to get."

"I don't want your damn money, Jillian."

"I know that. Have always known it." She turned pleading eyes to his. "It's not about money. It's never really been about money. That's my mother's game, not mine. It's about not trusting myself to believe that I can be enough to hold anyone . . . to hold you. The survival instincts have crippled me, Reese, until I'm afraid to ever reach for anything risky again. That way I'm sure not to lose."

He turned to face her, and her heart caught in her throat. Dear God she loved this man.

"What are you telling me, Jillian?"

It was now or never. Jillian closed the gap between them.

"I'm telling you I'm a stupid fool. I'm telling you how sorry I am that I hurt you. It is the very last thing I ever wanted to do."

Reese stiffened and stepped back. Jillian felt a draft creep into her heart at the cold expression that crossed his face. She was going to lose him.

"Apology accepted." He began to turn, but she grabbed his arm, yanking as hard as she could. Caught off guard he spun on his heel and stumbled into her.

Jillian steadied him by grasping his shoulders, then lifted her hands to his head and pulled it down to hers.

She kissed him hard. Her heart, her life, her soul, everything was in that kiss. He tensed, accepting the fierce pressure of her mouth on his.

But he didn't respond.

Tears gathered in the corners of her eyes as she gentled the kiss, turning it from a declaration to a good-bye. Finally she dropped her hands and he lifted his head.

She looked up at him. "I don't know what else to say. How else to apologize for what I did." The tears began to trickle down her cheeks. "Being scared was no excuse. I was wrong."

His expression darkened. "Bloody hell, I heard you the first time. Now can I go?"

She was handling this so badly. He wasn't hearing what she was saying. "That's what I'm trying to tell you, Reese. I don't want you to go. I never wanted you to go."

It took a second, then his expression changed to one of wariness. "What exactly are you saying? Spell it out."

"I'm saying that if you still want me, take me. I love you, Reese. Don't leave me. Don't ever leave me. And I swear I will never, ever, turn you away."

"Say that again," he commanded, his expression still fierce.

"I didn't want you to go. But I knew I wouldn't survive loving you and losing you later on. Better to lose you now."

"You will never lose me, Jillian." He kissed her so hard, it hurt. And the pain was a wonderful benediction. "You may wish you could, but your fate is sealed."

"Thank God," she said fervently through her

sniffles. Then laughed helplessly when he smiled and the sniffles turned to great gulping sobs.

He pulled her tight against his chest, holding her head against his heartbeat.

"I'm sorry . . . I can't seem . . . to stop . . ." She took a shuddering breath. "It's just I'm so—"

Reese tilted her face up to his. Two tears tracked down his face. "I know, mite. I know."

She laughed and cried and hugged him again. "What a pair of no-hopers we are, huh?"

"Jillian?" His voice was sweetly hoarse.

"Mmmm?" She nuzzled more deeply into his embrace, sighing happily when he tightened his arms around her.

"You told me once. Tell me again." He leaned down and pressed his damp lips to her ear. "I need to hear you tell me again."

She smiled and looked up into his face. "I love you, Reese Braedon. For better, for worse. For always."

Pain filled his eyes along with renewed brightness.

"What's wrong? Reese?"

"I see what you mean. It is scary. Trusting that love, I mean. But I do. I do."

"I know. After being alone inside for so long it's hard to let someone else in. To really believe they'll stay no matter what."

"You're inside me, Jillian. Always. I feel connected to you in a way I don't even understand.

And I don't care. You're part of me. The best part. Don't leave. Just don't ever leave."

She hugged him, then when that wasn't enough, she pulled his head back down and kissed him again. Only this time it wasn't one-sided.

Reese backed her up against the counter, then lifted her to sit on top of it. Her shirt was half off, her mind half gone, when she whispered, "Tell me, Reese. Tell me."

He bared one breast and took his sweet, torturous time kissing it, then slowly bared the other and gave it the same mind-bending attention. Then he wound slow, hot, wet kisses along her collar and up her neck until she'd forgotten what she'd asked him.

Until he got to the soft tender spot just below her ear.

"I love you, Jillian. For better, for worse. For always." He pulled her earlobe into his mouth and sucked on it. She gasped. He smiled.

"This," he whispered as he pulled her legs around his waist. He moved his hips against her. "Does it hurt, mite?"

"Worse," she panted.

"Then let me make it better."

"Always?"

Clothes were hastily readjusted, and Reese grabbed her hips and lifted her. Slowly, exquisitely, he pulled her onto him. And when he was deeply inside of her, he smiled and whispered, "You know it, mite. You know it."

THE EDITOR'S CORNER

Spring is on its way, and with it come four wonderful new LOVESWEPTs. You'll want to lose yourself in these terrific stories with funny, interesting and sexy characters written by some of the most talented authors writing women's fiction today.

Starting things off is the ever-popular Charlotte Hughes with **HUSBAND WANTED,** LOVESWEPT #734. Fannie Brisbane knows it is an impossible scheme, but unless she agrees to it, the daughter she gave up for adoption years ago will know the truth, that she's not rich and married! Her Griddle and Grill customers all pitch in, offering clothes, even a mansion—but when Clay Bodine offers to play her husband, Fannie doesn't know if she should dare say yes to a charade with the man who's always owned her heart. With her trademark humor and unforgettable characters, Charlotte delivers another sweetly sizzling romance that resonates with tenderness and sparkles with fun.

Linda Cajio's heroine has found **THE PERFECT CATCH,** LOVESWEPT #735. Elaine Sampson cheers joyfully, waving her arms as the player rounds the bases—and drenches the gorgeous guy in front of her with ice and cola! Graham Reed accepts her apology, but when the pretty teacher follows him to the men's room to help clean his suit, he laughs . . . and wonders if he is falling in love. He makes her reckless, kisses her senseless, but this handsome hunk might be a little out of her league. Linda's delightful love story hits an out-of-the-park home run!

Welcome Faye Hughes, a wonderfully talented new writer debuting at Loveswept with **CAN'T FIGHT THE FEELING,** LOVESWEPT #736. It took Justin Stone five minutes to fall in love with Morgan Tremayne—and nearly six years to recover from their quickie divorce ten months later! Now Morgan is back—flirting, teasing, igniting desires that have never really died—and determined to show her beloved pirate that she is his destiny. Once he wooed her with poetry and kisses that melted her clothes off, but now he wants to claim his fallen angel at last. Wildly sexy and delightfully outrageous, this sensational novel by Faye will enchant readers with a story that's as playful as it is seductive.

Last but not least is the fabulous Linda Warren with **AFTER MIDNIGHT,** LOVESWEPT #737. Cord Prescott never asks if Arianna Rossini is guilty when he comes to bail her out of jail, but something unspoken passes between them and tells him she didn't embezzle the missing money. But when she asks for a deal instead of a trial, he aches to learn her secrets, to persuade her to surrender the truth. Consumed by desire, haunted by guilt, Ari must help Cord make peace with his own demons. In a novel that's all at once provocative, passionate, and poignant, Linda explores a forbidden love between a rebel attorney who's won everything but a woman's heart and a lady whose mystery may be innocence or deceit.

Happy reading!

With warmest wishes,

Beth de Guzman   Shauna Summers

Senior Editor   Assistant Editor

P.S. Don't miss the women's novels coming your way in April: **MISTRESS,** by Amanda Quick, is the terrific *New York Times* bestseller, in paperback for the first time; **DANGEROUS TO KISS,** by the award-winning Elizabeth Thornton, is an unforgettable historical romance in the tradition of Amanda Quick and Jane Feather, set in Regency England; **LONG NIGHT MOON,** by highly acclaimed author

Theresa Weir, is a gripping and emotional romance in which a brash reporter helps an ethereal beauty escape a harrowing life. And immediately following this page, look for a preview of the exciting romances from Bantam that are *available now!*

Don't miss these fantastic books by your favorite Bantam authors

On sale in February:

NIGHT SINS
by Tami Hoag

THE FOREVER TREE
by Rosanne Bittner

MY GUARDIAN ANGEL ANTHOLOGY
by Kay Hooper
Sandra Chastain
Susan Krinard
Karyn Monk
Elizabeth Thornton

PAGAN BRIDE
by Tamara Leigh

"A master of the genre."
—*Publishers Weekly*

NIGHT SINS

by

TAMI HOAG

Available in Hardcover

Every once in a while a thriller comes along that stretches the limits of the genre and takes readers places they have never been before. Night Sins *is such a novel. . . .*

Deer Lake is a small Minnesota town where people know their neighbors and crime is something that happens on the evening news. But the illusion of safety is shattered when eight-year-old Josh Kirkwood disappears from a hockey rink as he waits for his mother to pick him up after practice. The only thing the police find is his duffel bag with a note stuffed inside: ignorance is not innocence but SIN.

The following is a chilling preview of what transpires the night Hannah realizes her son is missing.

"I forgot. I forgot he was waiting."
A fresh wave of tears washed down Hannah's

cheeks and fell like raindrops onto the lap of her long wool skirt. She doubled over, wanting to curl into a ball while the emotions tore at her. Mitch leaned closer and stroked her hair, trying to offer some comfort. The cop in him remained calm, waiting for facts, reciting the likely explanations. Deeper inside, the parent in him experienced a sharp stab of instinctive fear.

"When I g-got to the rink he w-was g-gone."

"Well, honey, Paul probably picked him up—"

"No. Wednesday is *my* night."

"Did you call Paul to check?"

"I tried, but he wasn't in the office."

"Then Josh probably got a ride with one of the other kids. He's probably at some buddy's house—"

"No. I called everyone I could think of. I checked at the sitter's—Sue Bartz. I thought maybe he would be there waiting for me to come pick up Lily, but Sue hadn't seen him." And Lily was still there waiting for her mother, probably wondering why mama had come and gone without her. "I checked at home, just in case he decided to walk. I called the other hockey moms. I drove back to the rink. I drove back to the hospital. *I can't find him.*"

"Do you have a picture of your son?" Megan asked as she came around the desk.

"His school picture. It's not the best—he needed a haircut, but there wasn't time." Hannah pulled her purse up onto her lap. Her hands shook as she dug through the leather bag for her wallet. "He brought the slip home from school and I made a note, but then time just got away from me and I— forgot."

She whispered the last word as she opened to the

photograph of Josh. *I forgot.* Such a simple, harmless excuse. Forgot about his picture. Forgot about his haircut. Forgot him. Her hand trembled so badly she could barely manage to slip the photograph from the plastic window. She offered it to the dark-haired woman, realizing belatedly that she had no idea who the woman was.

"I'm sorry," she murmured, dredging up the ingrained manners and a fragile smile. "Have we met?"

Mitch sat back against the edge of the desk again. "I'm sorry, Hannah. This is Agent O'Malley with the Bureau of Criminal Apprehension. Megan, this is Dr. Hannah Garrison, head of the emergency room in our community hospital. One of the best doctors ever to wield a stethoscope," he added with a ghost of a grin. "We're very lucky to have her."

Megan studied the photograph, her mind on business, not social niceties. A boy of eight or nine wearing a Cub Scout uniform stared out at her. He had a big gap-toothed grin and a smattering of freckles across his nose and cheeks. His hair was an unruly mop of sandy brown curls. His blue eyes were brimming with life and mischief.

"Is he normally a pretty responsible boy?" Megan asked. "Does he know to call you if he's going to be late or to get permission to go to a friend's house?"

Hannah nodded. "Josh is very levelheaded."

"What did he wear to school today?"

Hannah rubbed a hand across her forehead, trying to think back to morning. It seemed as much a dream as any of this, long ago and foggy. Lily crying at the indignity of being confined to her high chair. Josh skating around the kitchen floor in his stocking feet. Permission slip needed signing for a field trip to the Science Museum. Homework done? Spelling words memorized? A call from the hospital. French toast burning on the stove. Paul storming around the kitchen, snapping at Josh, complaining about the shirts that needed ironing.

"Um—jeans. A blue sweater. Snow boots. A ski jacket—bright blue with bright yellow and bright green trim. Um . . . his Viking stocking cap—it's yellow with a patch sewn on. Paul wouldn't let him wear a purple one with that wild coat. He said it would look like Josh was dressed by color-blind gypsies. I couldn't see the harm; he's only eight years old . . ."

Megan handed the photograph back and looked up at Mitch. "I'll call it in right away." Her mind was already on the possibilities and the steps they should take in accordance with those possibilities. "Get the bulletin to your people, the sheriff's department, the highway patrol—"

Hannah looked stricken. "You don't think—"

"No," Mitch interceded smoothly. "No, honey, of course not. It's just standard procedure. We'll put out a bulletin to all the guys on patrol so if they see Josh they'll know to pick him up and bring him home.

"Excuse us for just a minute," he said, holding up a finger. He turned his back to Hannah and a furious look to Megan. "I need to give Agent O'Malley a few instructions."

He clamped a hand on Megan's shoulder and herded her unceremoniously out the door and into the narrow, dimly-lit hall. A round-headed man in a tweed blazer and chinos gave them a dirty look and stuck a finger in his free ear as he tried to have a conversation on a pay phone outside the men's room door. Mitch hit the phone's plunger with two fingers, cutting off the conversation and drawing an indignant "Hey!" from the caller.

"Excuse us," Mitch growled, flashing his badge. "Police business."

He shouldered the man away from the phone and sent him hustling down the hall with a scowl that had scattered petty drug pushers and hookers from the meanest streets in Miami. He turned the same scowl on Megan. He towered over her and had to outweigh her by a good eighty pounds. He had physically intimidated men who were twice her size and mean as alligators. Yet she glared right back at him.

"What the hell is wrong with you?" she snapped, jumping on the offensive, knowing it was her best defense. She could feel his temper, a physical heat that seared her skin.

"What the hell is wrong with me?" Mitch barked, keeping his voice low. "What the hell is wrong with you—scaring the poor woman—"

"She has reason to be scared, Chief. Her son is missing."

"That has yet to be established. He's probably playing at a friend's house."

"She says she checked with his friends."

"Yes, but she's panicked. She's probably forgotten to look in an obvious place."

"Or somebody grabbed the kid."

Mitch scowled harder because it took an effort to

dismiss her suggestion outright. "This is Deer Lake, O'Malley, not New York."

Megan arched a brow. "You don't have crime in Deer Lake? You have a police force. You have a jail. Or is that all just window dressing?"

"Of course we have crime," he snarled. "We have college students who shoplift and cheese factory workers who get drunk on Saturday night and try to beat each other up in the American Legion parking lot. We don't have child abductions, for Christ's sake."

"Yeah, well, welcome to the nineties, Chief," she said sarcastically. "It can happen anywhere."

"Power, passion, tragedy, and triumph are Rosanne Bittner's hallmarks. Again and again, she brings readers to tears."
—*Romantic Times*

THE FOREVER TREE
by
Rosanne Bittner

Against the glorious, golden land of California, award-winning Rosanne Bittner creates another sweeping saga of passion, tragedy, and adventure . . . as a Spanish beauty and a rugged New Englander struggle against all odds to carve out an empire—and to forge a magnificent love.

Here is a look at this powerful novel.

Señorita Lopez, what are you doing here alone?"

"I often come here," Santana answered. "*Mi padre* lets me go riding alone, as long as it is only to this place that I love." She looked up at the lone pine tree. "I hope that you would never cut this tree, or those around it that protect and shelter it. I feel sorry for it. It seems so alone here, so I come to keep it company. I call it my forever tree."

"The forever tree. Why is that?"

She shrugged. "When I think about how old the California pines become, and how young this one still is, I know it will be here for a very long time, long after I die, even though I am only sixteen." Will saw a shadow of sadness cross her face. "So many things in life change as we grow older, but a tree is forever, a sign that some things never have to change."

He frowned, touched by the way she described the tree as something with a heart and soul. That was how he felt about trees himself, that they were a form of living poetry, something strong yet warm, something that gave so many things to man—shade, homes, paper, the warmth of a wood fire . . . "I'm glad to know you love trees as much as I do," he answered. He was sure he was not supposed to be alone with her this way, but he didn't care. She wore no veil, no special jewelry. Like the day she had come to his room, she was simply dressed. She needed nothing to add to her beauty.

"I love trees very much, *señor*, and the birds, the animals . . ."

Will smiled. "I wish you would just call me Will."

Santana felt a flush coming to her cheeks. "It is best that I do not," she said, smiling shyly. "Well, perhaps whenever I see you alone this way."

Will wondered if that meant she wanted to meet alone with him more often. That did not seem wise, but then, she was too young to be wise, and he was too enamored with her when she was near like this to care about doing the wise thing himself. "Good," he answered. "I have enjoyed getting to know you and your family, Santana. May I call you Santana?"

"*Si*, when we are alone."

Will looked her over, thinking how lovely her naked body must be under her dark riding habit. "I doubt that will happen very often."

She shrugged. "I suppose not. You will be very busy soon with building your mill, and I will be busy with my schooling, and with preparing myself for marriage."

He caught the bitterness in her words. "Surely you don't really want to marry Hugo Bolivar."

She turned away. "That is a forbidden subject."

Will sighed. "All right then, what *can* we talk about?" A little voice warned him that he should get on his horse and ride hell-bent out of there. A stronger force, though, made him stay. For more than two weeks now he had argued with himself that he should keep out of this woman's business, but every time he saw her at meals, listened to her talk, realized what a lovely and innocent woman-child she was, he felt anger and frustration at the thought of her becoming Hugo's wife.

Their eyes met. "*Gracias*," she said. "You are a very nice man, Will Lassater. I like talking with you. You make it easy. I can never find anything to talk about with Hugo. He only likes to talk about himself and his riches." She looked away, realizing she had said something she had not meant to say. "I suppose I will get used to him. Once he is my husband, we will have many things to talk about, and there will be children to share."

A pain stabbed through Will's gut at the thought

of Bolivar bedding Santana. He had no doubt the man would be rough and demanding. "You don't really want to marry that man and have children by him, do you?"

Santana rose, walking a few feet away. "I told you I cannot talk about that. I should not have even mentioned him."

"Nobody knows we're talking about it. Something tells me you *need* to talk about it, Santana. Probably nobody else you know understands how much you detest marrying Hugo. They all think you should be honored and privileged to marry such a man. But you don't want to, do you?"

MY GUARDIAN ANGEL

Five bewitching tales of romance from
**Sandra Chastain   Kay Hooper
Susan Krinard   Karyn Monk
Elizabeth Thornton**

ALMOST AN ANGEL by Kay Hooper
A handsome British agent won't rest until he finds the beautiful stranger who miraculously rescued him—then vanished as quickly as she appeared.

GUARDIAN OF THE HEART by Sandra Chastain
A brave young widow is left alone to fend for herself on the banks of the Rio Grande, until the ghost of her husband brings her a second chance at love.

ANGEL ON MY SHOULDER by Susan Krinard
A lovely actress torn from her lover's arms finds that her beloved pet, a wily parrot, houses a spirit determined to see that the two meet again.

SAVING CELESTE by Karyn Monk
A Bostonian with a tragic past prevents a despairing young woman from throwing herself off a bridge, and discovers that she holds the key to his happiness.

THE TROUBLE WITH ANGELS
by Elizabeth Thornton
The rakish young footman from Dangerous to Love makes a reappearance, this time dancing attendance on a spoiled beauty bent on landing a titled husband. It's all Flynn can do to keep his charge's reputation intact—and his hands to himself.

PAGAN BRIDE

by

Tamara Leigh

Bound by the chains of slavery in an exotic land, Lucien de Gautier had only one chance of escape. In exchange for his freedom, he pledged to smuggle a virtuous young woman out of a harem and onto a ship bound for England. But Lucien couldn't know that the real danger would lie not in the long voyage ahead, but in his dazzling charge: a ravishing innocent whose flame-red hair and emerald eyes would unleash his most potent desires. . . .

The music grew louder, its vigorous beat coursing through every vein in every limb that moved to it. Tightly, it wound itself around the slender woman who swayed at the center of the large room. It pulled her head back and closed her eyes against the light. It drew her arms up from her sides and spread them wide to embrace the sensual rhythm she had given herself over to. It shook her shoulders, rotated and jerked her hips, and caused her fingers to snap.

The female dancers who had been hired to entertain the women of Abd al-Jabbar's harem drifted away, going to stand along the walls and watch this strange one who had joined in the dance.

She was different from the other women, her hair a flame amid the ashes. Skin that should have been pale was tanned and faintly touched with freckles. Though fine-boned and slim, her body curved where it ought to, her breasts full and firm. And those pale green eyes—they were full of daring and laughter when she turned them upon her captive audience.

All watched as the tempo quickened and the solitary dancer swept across the floor, sparkling laughter spilling from her throat as the music pulled her deeper into its spell.

Unmindful of the pins holding her veil in place, the young woman snatched the translucent material from her waist-length hair and drew it taut between her hands. Then, raising her arms above her head, she pivoted on the balls of her bare feet. Faster and faster she turned, until she whirled in the wake of the diaphanous material clothing her limbs.

More laughter parted her lips, followed by a shriek of delight as the music reached its zenith. She was lost in it—completely given over to its control.

"Alessandra!" A reproving voice split the air.

The music fell away, and a din of women's voices rose to take its place.

Wrenched from the trancelike state she had slipped into, Alessandra staggered around to face her mother's displeasure. However, the room continued to revolve as if she were still dancing.

She sank to her knees and sat back on her heels, the dizziness making it impossible for her to focus on the woman who stood at the far end of the room.

Standing betwen Sabine and Khalid, Lucien knew he was in trouble. He had known the moment Sabine had called out to the wild dancer, naming her the one. Inwardly, he groaned and cursed his man's flesh. One look at the young woman as she whirled across the floor was all it had taken to decide him. Thinking her a dancer—though with her mother's hair falling down her back, he should have known otherwise—he had determined to have her as soon as possible. Then the accursed woman at his side had shattered the possibility. Or had she?

And don't miss these outstanding romances from Bantam Books, on sale in March:

MISTRESS
Available in paperback
by the *New York Times* bestselling author
Amanda Quick
"Amanda Quick is one of the most versatile and talented authors of the decade."
—*Romantic Times*

DANGEROUS TO KISS
by the award-winning
Elizabeth Thornton
"A major, major talent . . . a superstar."
—*Romantic Times*

LONG NIGHT MOON
by the incomparable
Theresa Weir
"Theresa Weir's writing is poignant, passionate and powerful."
—Jayne Ann Krentz

*To enter the sweepstakes outlined below, you must respond by the date specified and
follow all entry instructions published elsewhere in this offer.*

DREAM COME TRUE SWEEPSTAKES

Sweepstakes begins 9/1/94, ends 1/15/96. To qualify for the Early Bird Prize, entry must be received by the date specified elsewhere in this offer. Winners will be selected in random drawings on 2/29/96 by an independent judging organization whose decisions are final. Early Bird winner will be selected in a separate drawing from among all qualifying entries.

Odds of winning determined by total number of entries received. Distribution not to exceed 300 million.

Estimated maximum retail value of prizes: Grand (1) $25,000 (cash alternative $20,000); First (1) $2,000; Second (1) $750; Third (50) $75; Fourth (1,000) $50; Early Bird (1) $5,000. Total prize value: $86,500.

Automobile and travel trailer must be picked up at a local dealer; all other merchandise prizes will be shipped to winners. Awarding of any prize to a minor will require written permission of parent/guardian. If a trip prize is won by a minor, s/he must be accompanied by parent/legal guardian. Trip prizes subject to availability and must be completed within 12 months of date awarded. Blackout dates may apply. Early Bird trip is on a space available basis and does not include port charges, gratuities, optional shore excursions and onboard personal purchases. Prizes are not transferable or redeemable for cash except as specified. No substitution for prizes except as necessary due to unavailability. Travel trailer and/or automobile license and registration fees are winners' responsibility as are any other incidental expenses not specified herein.

Early Bird Prize may not be offered in some presentations of this sweepstakes. Grand through third prize winners will have the option of selecting any prize offered at level won. All prizes will be awarded. Drawing will be held at 204 Center Square Road, Bridgeport, NJ 08014. Winners need not be present. For winners list (available in June, 1996), send a self-addressed, stamped envelope by 1/15/96 to: Dream Come True Winners, P.O. Box 572, Gibbstown, NJ 08027.

THE FOLLOWING APPLIES TO THE SWEEPSTAKES ABOVE:

No purchase necessary. No photocopied or mechanically reproduced entries will be accepted. Not responsible for lost, late, misdirected, damaged, incomplete, illegible, or postage-die mail. Entries become the property of sponsors and will not be returned.

Winner(s) will be notified by mail. Winner(s) may be required to sign and return an affidavit of eligibility/release within 14 days of date on notification or an alternate may be selected. Except where prohibited by law, entry constitutes permission to use of winners' names, hometowns, and likenesses for publicity without additional compensation. Void where prohibited or restricted. All federal, state, provincial, and local laws and regulations apply.

All prize values are in U.S. currency. Presentation of prizes may vary; values at a given prize level will be approximately the same. All taxes are winners' responsibility.

Canadian residents, in order to win, must first correctly answer a time-limited skill testing question administered by mail. Any litigation regarding the conduct and awarding of a prize in this publicity contest by a resident of the province of Quebec may be submitted to the Regie des loteries et courses du Quebec.

Sweepstakes is open to legal residents of the U.S., Canada, and Europe (in those areas where made available) who have received this offer.

Sweepstakes in sponsored by Ventura Associates, 1211 Avenue of the Americas, New York, NY 10036 and presented by independent businesses. Employees of these, their advertising agencies and promotional companies involved in this promotion, and their immediate families, agents, successors, and assignees shall be ineligible to participate in the promotion and shall not be eligible for any prizes covered herein.　SWP 3/95